INTO THE BEWILDERNESS

A SHORT STORY COLLECTION

JOHN W. OTTE

GEEKY GRACE BOOKS

For the OYANers
Because when I think of fun,
I think of you guys

CONTENTS

FOREWORD

This book was born out of desperation.

One of my favorite things to do is teach at the One Year Adventure Novel conference, which is held in Olathe, Kansas. The students I meet there are absolutely phenomenal. They are so enthusiastic and creative and just so much fun. And when I go to the conference, I get to sell a few books as well, which is always a plus.

The first two years I went, I had stacks of my novels to bring along. But in 2018, I had no new books to bring along. None. Nothing. And I wanted to have something new to offer the students. So I wracked my brain and thought about it. And I realized I had about a dozen short stories sitting around, just waiting to be anthologized. So I took a crash course on how to format a book via Word (I do not recommend this method), got a quick cover, and threw together the first edition of *Into the Bewilderness.*

Here's what I wrote in the original foreword of the first edition:

This is unusual territory for me.

I'm not much of a short story kind of guy. I tend to struggle with reigning in my instincts when it comes to story length, preferring to go for overly large tales and books. So it's strange for me to sometimes dip my toes into the waters of short fiction.

But occasionally I've done it. I did it when I started on my journey toward publication (The Jewel of Creation and Irruption). I've written shorter pieces for anthologies (Satisfaction Guaranteed, The Night Queen, Like Manna from the Heavens, and Homecoming). I've dabbled in flash fiction (Focal Point and In the Shadow). And lately, I've even had to stretch beyond my comfort zone thanks to the NYC Midnight Short Story Challenge (the last four stories in this book).

After my journeys through these stories, I wanted to share them with you too. So enjoy getting lost in the bewilderness with me for a little while. You never know what you might find.

Yikes. I know, right?

So why a second edition? Well, for a couple of reasons. For starters, I never liked the way the formatting turned out for the first edition. I made a lot of weird mistakes that I was never able to fix. I've got better software now, so I figured I would redo the formatting for both ebook and print.

Second, I always thought it might be fun to include some notes with each story, giving some behind-the-scenes insight into where the stories came from. Maybe you'll find that interesting and maybe you won't.

So happy reading!

THE JEWEL OF CREATION

KING AMBRUS—DESCENDED OF GODS, Divine Son of a Divine Father, the Ever-Correct and Never-Failing, Protector of the Holy City of Sakan, Ruler of All Davaru, Destined Emperor of the World—lounged on his throne, giggling in his high-pitched voice as a young boy massaged his feet and an even younger girl braided his long, honey-gold hair.

His courtiers fanned out through the gilded throne room, observing the young despot, careful to keep their expressions neutral. While the king's emerald eyes shone with giddy delight now, a mistimed whisper or a misunderstood look could cause them to flare with deadly anger. Too many people had been executed for such "treason" over the years.

But today they could relax. Ambrus had already selected a victim for his godly wrath and had anticipated the trial for days. It would take a *faux pas* of monumental proportions to incur his wrath, so focused was Ambrus on destroying his latest nemesis. The courtiers were grateful for the chance to relax in the presence of their king, but they also felt sorry for Ambrus's next victim. Most knew and respected General Batair. Seeing him disgraced and disposed of in such a dishonorable way saddened them. At the same time, though, most felt a certain measure of relief that they weren't the ones who had "failed" the king.

The massive doors to the throne room opened and a contingent of the royal guard, resplendent in their gold ceremonial armor, trooped through. A nervous whisper rippled through the gathered courtiers. General Batair's straight posture and lifted chin made him seem to tower over the guards even though he was a handbreadth shorter than them. The guards came to a halt in the center of the room.

"General Elias Batair, as ordered, Ineffable One," the captain of the guard announced, and then he and his men marched back to their posts.

Ambrus ignored Batair at first, cooing in delight at the slaves who ministered to him. The general remained stoic. Ambrus was impressed. Even though the general had been locked in a dank dungeon for two weeks, he looked none the worse for wear. His face, though creased with lines, looked noble instead of aged. His hair, a halo of white, lent dignity to his appearance. Batair almost appeared as if he should be standing on a pedestal for future generations to admire.

Yigol, Ambrus's High Counselor, stepped forward. Though Yigol and the king were nearly the same age, the High Counselor looked many years older. His sandy hair had already retreated from his pock-marked forehead. The large man wheezed as he leaned over to whisper something to the king. Ambrus rolled his eyes and shooed the boy and girl away.

"Ah, dear General." A snarl tugged at the corner of Ambrus's lips. "You do realize why I recalled you from the front, don't you?"

Batair didn't reply. He stared at Ambrus, his face still as stone.

"You dare to not answer?" Ambrus stretched on the throne. "But I suppose I shouldn't be surprised. You're here because of your defiance. This is just more of the same." He turned to Yigol. "Get on with it."

Yigol stalked down the stairs, never taking his eyes from Batair. The general ignored him. Finally, the High Counselor turned to the gathered courtiers.

"Attention, all those who bask in the Divine Presence. General Elias Batair is hereby on trial. The charge is..." Yigol paused dramatically. The courtiers collectively sucked in an appropriately nervous breath, even though they knew full well what the charge was.

"Treason," Yigol stated.

The courtiers, long adept at playacting for Ambrus, whispered to each other as if surprised. Ambrus allowed the murmur to grow for several moments before waving for silence. He nodded to Yigol.

The High Counselor turned back to the courtiers. "Now, some may wonder why the legendary General Batair, supposed hero of the Davaran people, would be charged with treason." He paused, allowing the audience to ask the appropriate question to each other. "After all, this is a man who has served in the army of three Divine Kings—starting as a lowly squire, clawing his way up through the ranks until he was placed in command of our mighty armies by the departed King Kladin, our august ruler's father. How could such a noble man come to such a lowly end?" Yigol took a step forward so he could look down his nose at Batair. "By failing the godly Ambrus and the Davaran people."

Another wave of whispers crescendoed in the gilded room. Yet Batair's first words cut through it all.

"How?"

Yigol flinched away from Batair. "How? How, you ask?" The High Counselor's head whirled towards the king, the Counselor's eyes wide and pleading. Ambrus's glare sent Yigol's gaze ricocheting back to Batair. Yigol sucked in a deep breath, straining his robes even more, before he continued. "Need I tell you? Ten years ago, after Ambrus ascended to the throne, he gave you but one task, one assignment that he expected you to complete. And what was that task?"

Batair didn't answer. Yigol turned to the crowd.

"Our Divine Majesty commanded this supposedly capable general to conquer our worst enemy and add their glory to ours. Our Beloved Deity ordered him to destroy Ledia."

A genuine gasp ripped through the crowd. All eyes were on Ambrus. He had forbidden anyone from speaking the name of the city of their worst enemy.

Ledia was legend. Reputed to be a center of incredible learning, a commercial hub unlike any other, rich beyond most people's dreams. Those who saw it understood why it was called the "Jewel of Creation."

For centuries, Ledia and Sakan were friendly rivals. However, during the reign of Ambrus's father, Kladin, that relationship soured. And when Kladin was murdered, supposedly by order of his rival, King Namtari of Ledia, Ambrus dedicated his life to breaking Ledia.

Normally the mere mention of Ledia's name was enough to send Ambrus into a blind fury, one that resulted in numerous executions.

Yigol bowed before the king. "Forgive my impertinence, your majesty."

"In this case, I shall be lenient." Ambrus waved for Yigol to continue.

The high counselor turned back to Batair. "A full decade was given you, General Batair, yet Ledia still stands. For this, you stand accused of treason. How do you plead?"

Batair tilted his head back and peered down his nose at Yigol. "Plead? Why should I plead? His highness has no quarrel with me." The king shifted in his throne, and Batair added, "If you insist. I plead not guilty."

"Very well. Let the record show that the defendant has plead 'not guilty'," Yigol declared with a dramatic sweep of his arms. The courtiers exchanged unsure glances since no one was keeping a record.

Ambrus rapped the arm of his throne, prompting Yigol to freeze for a moment. He peeked back at the king, who glared at him.

"Your pardon, Divine One. I shall proceed." Yigol cleared his throat. "Your gall is remarkable, General. Pleading 'not guilty' when Ledia, the Jewel of Creation, still stands. What is worse, you have taken no steps to correct this affront to our king's divine honor. Let us review."

Yigol snapped his fingers, prompting a page to dart forward and press a roll of parchment into the High Counselor's hands. With a flick of his wrist, he unfurled the paper and glanced at it.

"Ten years ago, the king gave you gold to purchase the finest weapons for our army. Instead, you squandered it on expensive gifts that you sent overseas to rulers of foreign nations. Let's see here...Velanar, Chasway, Opletar. Perhaps you were trying to garner their favor in case you made a bid for Davaru's throne?

"Seven years ago, the king procured the finest military minds to both assist you with strategy and train your officers. You dismissed them and instead hired philosophers, artists, musicians, and other individuals unsuited for battle and proceeded to house them all at your estate.

"Six years ago, our Benevolent Deity brought you the finest wizards to incinerate the Ledians with magical fire and other such spells. You instead sent them to the Ledian hills where they apparently skulked

about for weeks and never came within sight of Ledia's walls. Then
you banished them all, making it impossible for the king to learn what
you had been up to."

Yigol paused for a moment, glancing at Batair. The general stared
through Ambrus. Yigol exchanged a glance with the king, then re-
ferred to the parchment.

"Five years ago, you marched the glorious Davaran army to the walls
of Ledia and challenged them to combat. As soon as the Ledian army
mustered itself, you ordered a retreat through the Valley of Shadows
even though you were evenly matched, thereby showing your cow-
ardice.

"Four years ago, you requested a small fortune to finance your
operations. You claimed it was to hire mercenaries. You did use half of
it on Irinor barbarians. But rather than throw them against the gates
of our enemies, you had them run around the northern countryside,
never capturing, always pillaging. And the other half of the king's
bounty? You used it to hire troubadours, bards, traveling musicians,
and poets. Did you keep those entertainers on your estate with your
philosophers and professors?

"And then just last year, you requested a corps of engineers. It was
assumed that after wasting so much time, you were finally going to
assault Ledia. Rather than have them build siege engines and weapon-
ry, you sent them on a nature walk through a mountain range thirty
leagues to the south of our loathed enemy."

Yigol, who had been pacing between Ambrus and Batair, came to a
halt and waved the parchment under the general's nose. Batair leaned
back ever so slightly, just enough to avoid getting hit.

"I could go on, General," Yigol shouted, imbuing the last word
with as much sarcasm as he could muster. "There's more, but I don't
want to bore these good people with your failures. The points I've

mentioned prove your treason well enough. You should have destroyed Ledia by now, as our Ineffable Ruler decreed. You have failed, wasting time and resources in defiance of our Lord's commands. Therefore, you are guilty of treason."

Yigol sketched a short bow to Batair, a mocking smile splitting his face. He backed away, then turned to Ambrus, who smiled in satisfaction.

"I would say the High Counselor's conclusions are well-nigh undeniable. Do you have anything to say in your defense, Elias?"

Batair's spine stiffened at the king's familiarity, but the tension quickly bled away. He locked a fiery glare on Ambrus.

"I have always considered myself a loyal son of Davaru. My fealty has never been in question before. When my king, no matter who he was, requested my services, I gave it without question, knowing full well that I may be asked to sacrifice my life for the glory and honor of Sakan and all Davaru. It is a pity I must sacrifice it now."

"That is your defense?" Yigol asked, his voice incredulous.

"Why should I defend myself? You and I both know how this will end. What I say will make little difference. I have accepted that. This...farce was put on for your amusement, not in a search for justice, and we both know it, Ambrus."

Several of the courtiers shrieked. No one had permission to use the king's name. Yigol paled and shrank away as the king exploded from the throne.

"How dare you!" Ambrus thundered.

"What do I have to lose? We both know how this will end and nothing I say will change that."

The king's anger suddenly melted into a crafty smile. "So you realize your guilt then? Do you wish to change your plea? If you admit your treason, I may show lenience."

Batair laughed, turning to the courtiers. "Do any of you believe that Ambrus knows what 'lenience' means? It's clear he has no concept of justice."

"You insult your king?"

"You are only my king because your father didn't sire any other children. If he had, you would be nothing more than a spoiled prince in the court of your vastly superior sibling."

Ambrus sputtered, but Batair didn't give him a chance to speak. "You asked for my defense and I shall give it. I am not guilty for I have not failed you."

Ambrus stared at Batair, his mouth slack. "Wh-what?"

"Ten years ago, you charged me with capturing Ledia. I believe your exact words were, 'Dear General, bring me the Jewel of Creation and I shall be eternally in your debt.'"

"I know what I said," Ambrus growled. "Everyone knows that Ledia still stands to this day. Travelers who cross the Eastern Plains speak of how its walls still shine from its mountain heights. How dare you claim you accomplished this task?"

"But I have. As you requested, I have brought you the Jewel of Creation. If you would ever leave the walls of your palace, you would understand that. Counselor Yigol, if you would do your job as you should rather than fawn over the king, you would come to realize it as well. Ledia is yours, Majesty."

"I've heard enough." Ambrus nodded to his guards. "Take him away. Regardless of what he says, he is guilty, and he stands here condemned to death. That, Elias, is divine justice, whether you realize it or not." He turned to the guard. "Take him away. He will be beheaded at dawn."

Batair took a step forward, causing Ambrus to stumble back into his throne. The general clenched and unclenched his fists, anger flaring in his eyes. Finally, he took a step back. He bowed his head as the guards grabbed him by his arms.

Ambrus laughed.

"Cowardly in life and in death," he crowed.

Batair's head snapped up. He appeared about to speak. Instead, his head dropped to his chest as the guards wheeled him about and dragged him from the throne room.

The chill in the morning air hovered across the execution grounds, refusing to retreat from the sun. It caressed Ambrus's arms, puckering his flesh. He shuddered, drawing his robes tighter around him.

The king glanced at the crowd and saw his courtiers flanking him. Ambrus scanned their faces, almost hoping he would find some trace of disappointment or sorrow. It would give him an excuse to cull the herd a little, sending Batair's friends into death with him. Sadly, it appeared that Batair would die alone. The courtiers remained impassive.

The king then turned his attention to the opposite side of the grounds. Officers from the army stood at rigid attention, eyes fixed forward. Ambrus had chosen those most loyal to the general to witness his execution. He wanted them to understand who was truly in charge of the Davaran forces.

Yigol pranced up next to him.

"What news?" Ambrus whispered.

The High Counselor leaned in close. "My spies among the army report there are many who despise you for convicting Batair. As far as my sources can tell, none plot to rescue him this morning, though many wish to. There are rumors that Batair forbade any such attempts."

Ambrus frowned. "That doesn't make sense. Why not command his loyal officers to rescue him? What about the wizards he hired?"

"He exiled them six years ago."

Before Ambrus could respond, the crash of an immense gong announced the arrival of Elias Batair. Once again, the condemned general seemed to tower above his escorts. Instead of prison rags, Batair wore his uniform. The morning light glimmered from the gilded edges of his tunic, shining through the diamond studs on his collar that denoted his rank. Ambrus ground his teeth. On most generals, the dress uniform looked gaudy, reducing the men inside to mere dandies. In Batair's case, the man overwhelmed the uniform.

The guards marched Batair to a spot before the king. A smirk curled the king's lips. This was his favorite part of any execution. Tradition demanded that when the king attended, the condemned could plead for mercy. Over the years, Ambrus had basked in the groveling, the flattery, the pledge to fulfill any whim Ambrus might have. None of it ever worked; Ambrus never denied himself the joy of an execution. But it still felt good to hear what the doomed had to say. Ambrus particularly relished the idea of hearing Batair grovel. A warm shiver danced up his spine as he anticipated the broken general falling to his knees and pleading for a second chance.

Yet when Batair met Ambrus's eyes, there was no groveling or fear. Only sad resignation. The king and the general stared at one another for a few moments before Ambrus spoke. "Well?"

"What shall I say? We both know how this ends. I regret that I must lose my life in this fashion, but I do so knowing that I have never fallen short of my duty," Batair said. "If I must be sacrificed for the greater glory of this kingdom, then so be it."

"Very well," Ambrus said. "The sentence shall be carried out immediately. And Elias, keep this thought with you as you face your end: where you have failed, I shall succeed. I intend to lead my armies into glorious battle and finally conquer Ledia."

A sad smile split Batair's face. "I wish you luck, Ambrus. Just remember the orders you gave me when you reach Ledia's gates and remember my defense."

With that, the general turned smartly on his heel and strode to the chopping block, his head held high. He paused only for a moment to salute his gathered officers. The guards snared his arms to force him down to the block. Batair shrugged them off, kneeling down and stretching his neck out. The executioner cast an unsure glance at Ambrus, as if seeking permission to proceed. The king glared his answer. The executioner hefted the axe and brought it down quickly.

Ambrus winced, looking away. After waiting a few moments, he stood from his throne and crossed the grounds. The officers snapped back to attention at his approach, but Ambrus could see anger simmering in many eyes.

"Do not forget what you have seen here. General Batair died for his treachery. The ground still thirsts for traitors' blood." He brightened a bit. "But let us move on. In preparation for our glorious campaign against Ledia, you and all your men shall receive double your normal pay. As we plan our assault, you are also given furlough to visit your loved ones. Spend your time well, my friends, for we will soon march for the glory of Davaru and Sakan."

The officers saluted him before turning as one and marching from the field. Yigol slinked up to Ambrus's side. "Do you think it worked?" the king asked.

Yigol shrugged. "We shall see. The extra gold will buy the fealty of most. But I have men ready to arrest those who remain loyal to Batair's memory. Let them follow the steps of their beloved general."

A month passed. When the time came, the gates to the palace were thrown open and the army streamed through with Ambrus at its head. The citizens of Sakan lined the streets to wish the army well. The heady scent of incense, offered to appease the gods, hung heavy in the air.

Ambrus shifted in his saddle nervously. It had been years since he had last left the palace. His life was sequestered behind the stone walls, safe from assassins, grasping nobles, and his citizens. He tried to smile, his lips frozen in a half-grimace that he knew didn't look sincere, and waved, a limp shake of the wrist that somehow elicited cheers.

The procession snaked through the narrow streets. As it did, a frown furrowed Ambrus's brow. He had only seen Sakan from the castle's windows and what little he knew was described by his advisors. Yet as he studied the city, what he saw didn't match what he had pictured. It was larger, more vibrant. The people's faces weren't uniformly pale as they had been in the past. Now, a variety of hues met his eyes. Moreover, the outfits they wore were richer than he expected. His ministers had always described his subjects as living in abject squalor. He made a mental note to have someone flogged if they couldn't explain the disparity.

As they rounded a corner, Ambrus caught sight of something that brightened his mood. Sprawled over the second-most prominent hill in Sakan (the palace occupied the first) was Elias Batair's estate, a mansion that the king had always coveted to house a few choice concubines. He drank in the house's graceful lines, the well-groomed landscape...the crowds of men and women coming and going?

He waved Yigol to his side. The High Counselor, unsteady on his charger, trotted up. Ambrus nodded toward the estate.

"That is Batair's house, yes? Where only he and his wife lived?"

"It was, Divine Majesty."

"Then why do I see so many people on the grounds and none of them dressed for mourning?"

Yigol hesitated before admitting, "I...I don't know."

Ambrus fixed him with a harsh stare. "Why don't you find out?"

Yigol swallowed hard and motioned for a page to ride off and find the answer. Ambrus watched his High Counselor through narrowed eyes. He had hoped Yigol would have caught the hint and investigated this puzzle himself. Perhaps he would have Yigol interrogated about all the inconsistencies he had seen.

The procession continued, taking much longer than Ambrus had expected. He had planned on riding through the unwashed masses for less than an hour. This trip had already taken two hours and yet the main gate appeared a long way off. With each new step, the king became more and more agitated. It wasn't just the press of peasants on all sides. No, confusion over the situation grew with every moment. Sakan had always been glorious but it had never been this large. Where had all the people come from? So many citizens looking so well off, new houses and shops wherever he looked...it didn't seem possible.

The confusion only grew as they passed through the gates, for the city continued beyond them. Even newer buildings lined the cobblestone streets, ones that bustled with smiling people.

When the army finally reached the edge of Sakan, Ambrus was convinced he couldn't handle any more mysteries, yet he found himself confronted by another. The last time he had been out in the Davaran countryside was before his coronation ten years earlier. Back then, only a dozen or so farms had dotted the landscape surrounding Sakan and most of the landscape was lush hills. Now there was nothing but farms as far as the eye could see. As a matter of fact, it seemed like they would never leave farm country. The carefully cultivated fields stretched from horizon to horizon.

Several hours after leaving the city, the page returned to Ambrus's side.

"Well? What took you so long?" Ambrus snapped.

"Your pardon, Deific One. I would have returned sooner but I had trouble finding anyone who could understand me."

Yigol and Ambrus exchanged confused looks. "What do you mean?" the High Counselor asked.

"Many of the men and women couldn't understand my questions. I believe some spoke Leda, but I couldn't recognize most of the languages."

Ambrus's eyes narrowed as a feral grin turned up his lips. Leda was the language spoken by the citizens of Ledia. If there had been any doubt about Batair's treason, this dispelled it. Why else would he have Ledians at his estate?

"I finally found someone who could answer my questions, and she said that Batair ceded his property rights to something called the Divine University of Sakan."

The blank look Yigol shared with Ambrus made it clear that he didn't know what that was either. Ambrus ground his teeth together. Maybe he would just order Yigol flogged for his amusement. The High Counselor was proving to be worthless for anything else.

The march from Sakan to Ledia took a week and a half. The army eventually left the myriad of farmsteads that ringed Sakan for miles, but unfortunately, the strange puzzles followed them with every step. On the way, they discovered half a dozen new towns that, as far as Ambrus could tell, hadn't existed for more than two or three years. When they reached the border between Davaru and Ledia, they discovered that the boundary stones had been moved, giving Davaru an extra twenty miles of territory.

Even more puzzling was the lack of opposition. Only Davaran troops guarded the border. No enemy patrols crossed their path as they marched through Ledian territory. They saw only a few peasants on the journey, but no one seemed all that concerned by the presence of a foreign army on their soil. Ambrus, on edge since crossing into the enemy's holdings, chalked their indifference up to overconfidence. Ledia's mighty armies hadn't been defeated in a hundred generations. But soon this blight against Ambrus's divinity would lie broken at his feet.

Finally, Ledia came into view, nestled on its mountain perch and towering over the Eastern Plains. The entire army paused to drink in the sight. Ambrus let his gaze roam over his prize. A momentary twinge of doubt flitted through his mind. Hearing of the high walls and impenetrable gates in Sakan had been one thing. But seeing them himself, he wondered if his army even had a chance of capturing the Jewel of Creation.

He shook off his doubt and signaled for General Horris to join him. Horris, a stout man with a map of scars lining his cheeks and forehead, had been in charge of the eastern defenses, one of the few men who hadn't served under Batair. That alone made him the most trustworthy candidate to lead the army.

"General, send out the scouts and ready the ram. We assault Ledia on the morn," the king crowed, expecting a roar of approval from the troops within earshot.

Instead, he was met with deafening silence. Horris stared at him, hard and unblinking.

"Meaning no offense, sire, but you might consider a parley first," Horris finally said. "Who knows? The sight of your divine eminence might cow them into submission."

Ambrus fixed his new general with a steely look. "Are you questioning my inspired will, General? Do you wish to follow in your predecessor's footsteps?"

Horris's face betrayed no emotion as he turned and relayed the king's orders. Engineers set about assembling a massive ram while scouts sped forward to assess the situation.

The ram was assembled and the teams were ready to wheel it into position when the scouts returned with a very odd report. No patrols on the walls. The towers were dark and unoccupied. No lamps, no smoke, not even the smell of cooked rations. At this news, Horris's gaze shifted over the silent towers. It only bolstered Ambrus's confidence. The Ledian fools were brashly overconfident. They would pay dearly for that mistake.

Once again, Horris hesitated when Ambrus gave the order to attack. This time, however, the general corrected his mistake by relaying the king's order. A battalion of soldiers started up the circuitous road that led to Ledia's main gates, the ram a short distance behind them. Ambrus followed with his finest knights. The king was already envisioning how his victory would develop. The peons in front would protect the ram from any Ledian sallies. The ram would turn the gates to kindling. Then he and his knights, resplendent in shining armor, would charge through the gap and slaughter those within. Ledia would fall before his divine wrath and the Jewel of Creation would finally be his.

As the procession crept up the snaking path, Ambrus gripped the reins of his horse tighter and tighter. He could imagine the soldiers tightening their hands on spears and sword hilts. His eyes scanned the looming walls for any sign of the enemy. Worry and confidence warred within Ambrus. Might the lack of guards mean that he had taken them by surprise? How was that possible? Were they so confident in their defenses they didn't see the need to man the walls? Was that confidence justified?

As he drew closer and closer to the gates, Ambrus wished that he was back in Sakan, safe and secure in his palace. He even momentarily wished he hadn't executed Batair. The general would have known what to do.

With a crash that Ambrus felt through his chest, the ram slammed into the gates. But as it drew back, the King was horrified to see that the gates appeared unharmed. The wood wasn't even scratched.

Horris shouted for them to try again. They did, but with the same result. They were winding up for a third time when Ambrus heard it.

"Hey!"

Ambrus nearly leapt out of his saddle at the shout. His eyes flew to the battlements above the gate. Much to his surprise, a lone man peeked over the edge, glaring at the army below.

"Stop that. What do you think you're doing?" Ambrus looked at Horris, who only shrugged.

"If you wanted to come inside, why didn't you just say something? Hang on, I'll be right down."

The man disappeared. Anxious whispers rippled through the army, and the soldiers turned to Ambrus for guidance. The king stared at the battlements, unsure of what to say or even to think.

After a few minutes, a small door opened in the gate, one barely large enough for a man to slip through. Ambrus studied him carefully. He was obviously Ledian by his wide-set eyes and flat nose, obscured by grime and dust as they were. The man was cadaverously slender, hunched over, and swathed in filthy rags. He shambled forward, bowing to Ambrus stiffly.

"Welcome, King Ambrus," he said, attempting to draw himself up into a regal stance. The effect, unfortunately for him, proved comical. A snicker broke out in the ranks, and even Ambrus was tempted to join them. The man ignored it. "Would you care to join me inside the gates?"

Horris eased forward, his hand darting to his sword. The man glanced at him and smiled. "You are welcome as well, General Batair."

"Batair is dead, wretch," Ambrus growled.

Conflicted emotions cascaded over the other man's face. Ambrus noted sadness, anger, and relief. All flashed by in a split second before the man spoke again. "Pity. It's a shame he couldn't inspect his handiwork."

"What?" Ambrus asked. "What are you talking about?"

"Why don't you come inside and see for yourself?" The man motioned toward the door.

Ambrus laughed. "I'm assuming my army can't join me. What guarantee do I have that this isn't a trap?"

The man met his gaze. "You have my word. I guarantee it by my honor as Namtari, King of Ledia."

A buzz swept through the ranks behind Ambrus. He squinted at the man. Yes, it was true. Now he recognized the man from the images on Ledian coins. This was Namtari.

He gritted his teeth. No matter how odd he dressed, Namtari was still king of Ledia. As a fellow monarch, Ambrus was honor-bound to take him at his word.

Ambrus slid from his saddle. He, Yigol, and Horris walked past Namtari to the open doorway. Ambrus paused for a moment to take a deep breath and then crossed the threshold.

Namtari took the lead, guiding the three Davarans through a massive gatehouse. Ambrus stared at the arch that towered sixty feet over his head. The interior was lined with slitted windows, the type archers could use to rain arrows on their enemies. The windows appeared empty, but Ambrus braced himself for an assault anyway.

"So tell me, cousin," Ambrus finally said. "Why do you dress so poorly? Where is the royal raiment you are famed for?"

Namtari snorted. "Fancy robes and golden crowns matter little in Ledia anymore, cousin, thanks to General Batair. But you'll understand that soon enough."

They came to another set of massive doors, which were also shut. Namtari inspected them, then wrenched open a smaller door. He stepped aside and bowed. Ambrus smiled at Yigol. Finally! He had dreamed of this moment for as long as he could remember—stepping into Ledia, walking the streets that were rumored to be paved with precious stones, seeing the legendary architecture, accepting the reverent fear of the inhabitants. It was time for him to meet his destiny.

With that, Ambrus stepped through the gates, only to stop short at what met his eyes.

Ledia was in ruins. Husks of buildings stood before him like tombstones. Dusty, muddy roads snaked between them. A coat of grime covered everything. Rather than throngs of people, Ambrus spotted a few wretches, dressed far worse than Namtari, shuffling from ruin to ruin.

Yigol gasped as he joined his king. "What happened here?"

"According to my spies, Elias Batair happened." Bitterness crept into Namtari's voice. "It's a shame he's dead, Ambrus. That man defeated Ledia for you."

Ambrus stared at the wreckage, his mind refusing to accept what he saw.

"How..." he finally managed to whisper.

Namtari sighed, sitting down on a crumbled foundation. "Let's see. Ten years ago, Batair bribed our allies to stop trading with us. It wasn't like we couldn't live without Velanaran wine or Opletran silks and the other fripperies, but some of the richer subjects decided that they couldn't and left, settling mostly in Davaru since they could get those goods there. Without those subjects to tax, I was forced to make up the difference as best as I could.

"Then seven years ago, rumors started circulating that Batair had founded a university staffed by the finest scholars in the world. Our children went there in droves and were taught that Davaru was superior to Ledia. Needless to say, most of them stayed in Sakan.

"Six years ago, I threw a lavish festival to celebrate my dynasty's two hundredth anniversary, hoping to entice back the rich and the young. Unfortunately, the festivities were marred by unusual portents in the heavens that our wise men interpreted as signs of impending disaster, war, famine, and disease. Scared out of their minds, the rich and the young who remained left and took thousands of others with them. We didn't realize that the signs were created by Davaran wizards until it was too late.

"Batair challenged us to battle five years ago, but because of the 'omens' of the previous year, most of my army had deserted. I mustered what few troops we had for battle and we were actually heartened by Batair's retreat. We chased him through the Valley of Shadows without realizing that Batair had lined the canyon with his best archers. I lost three quarters of my men and barely escaped with my life. The few survivors decided Batair was a demon and followed their comrades in deserting. Not that I blame them.

"Then four years ago, Irinor barbarians ravaged our farmlands to the northwest. Without my army, there was no way to stop them. At the same time, hordes of bards traipsed through the villages and farms, singing of how the benevolent King Ambrus kept his peasants protected, and how the rolling, lush fields of Davaru waited to be tilled. The peasants, angry with me for six years of high taxes and scared from the omens and the barbarian raids, left to seek their fortunes within your borders. That decimated our food supply.

"And finally, last year, our water supply dried up. You see, cousin, we have no springs or wells here in Ledia. All of our water comes from mountain springs to the south of here, carried by underground aqueducts. We had always believed them to be safe, but somehow, General Batair learned of their existence and had them dammed. We tried to get by with rainwater reservoirs, but we don't get much rain on our mountain perch. Everyone left who could, leaving me and very few others clinging to old, tattered memories."

Numbness crept up Ambrus's legs and spine. He stared at the burned out buildings, his nostrils assaulted by the stench of dust and decay. Namtari stood and waved at the panorama.

"There you go, your Majesty. Batair's legacy. I hope you're satisfied. Feel free to take some rubble to parade through Sakan and then, if you don't mind, just leave us alone. Your people have done enough to us already."

With that, Namtari walked away, leaving the three Davarans to stare at the ruins. Finally, Horris shook his head, turned on his heel, and stormed through the open door. Yigol looked to his king and started to say something, but a sharp look from Ambrus silenced him. The High Counselor retreated through the gate as well.

Ambrus stood at the city gates, staring at the ruins of Ledia, as still as a statue. Then a tugging at his robe caught his attention. He looked down and saw a little girl, no older than ten, looking up at him. Her black hair hung in shaggy tendrils around her dirt-smudged face. She appeared so thin that a stiff wind could have broken her in half. Her eyes gleamed as she asked, "Are you really King Ambrus?"

Ambrus stared at her, not comprehending her words for a few seconds, before answering, "I am, child."

Delight shone in the girl's eyes. "Can you take me back to Sakan? Please? My mama, she wants to stay here, but we don't have any reason. We need to get out of here."

Ambrus tried to speak, but found he couldn't think of the right words to say. Thankfully, the child's mother called her name and rushed from one of the nearby ruined houses.

"Begging your pardon, m'lord." She stepped between the child and the king, hiding her daughter behind her dress. "She meant no disrespect."

"I...I understand," Ambrus said. "It must be hard to live here."

"It is at that." The woman sighed, then smiled sadly. "Perhaps the little one is right. There's nothing for us here. Maybe we will move to Sakan."

Ambrus nodded stiffly. "That may be wise."

"Aye, it probably is. There's so much for a person in Sakan. It is the Jewel of Creation, after all."

Much to the surprise of the mother and her daughter, King Ambrus—Descended of Gods, Divine Son of a Divine Father, the Ever-Correct and Never-Failing, Protector of the Holy City of Sakan, Ruler of All Davaru, Destined Emperor of the World—collapsed and wept like a child.

NOTES ON "THE JEWEL OF CREATION"

THIS ONE WAS ACTUALLY the first short story I ever published.

Way back when in 2007, I had this idea for a short story where a king would want to conquer an apparent utopia, only to learn that his general succeeded in a rather unconventional way. I was thrilled when the magazine chose to publish my story. But I was also kind of a jerk about it. The editor who was working with me wanted to reformat the story so that it would be more showing than telling. In my inexperience as an author, I refused to change the story's structure. Thankfully, they didn't cancel their offer.

The only other really cool thing I can share about this story is a little tidbit about the publisher. *Leading Edge* is published by Brigham Young University's Department of Linguistics and English Language. One of the most notable people to come out of that department is phenomenal fantasy author Brandon Sanderson. Years after *The Jewel of Creation* was published, I discovered Sanderson's writings and I've devoured everything he's written since then. When I learned that

Sanderson had attended BYU, I wondered if maybe, just maybe, he had something to do with *Leading Edge*. Had he maybe edited my story? Well, I went back and looked. While he did volunteer at the magazine while he was at BYU, Sanderson wasn't on staff when my story was published.

IRRUPTION

IT WAS NOT GOING to be a good night.

Charles checked and rechecked the straps on his synthetic mage-armor vest. His hands roamed from his chest to his belt, briefly touching the radio, the extra ammo clips, the stun grenades. His fingers caressed the magazine of the semi-automatic RD-440 which hung around his neck. Electric tingles snaked up his arm. The effects of the inhibium-jacketed bullets? He shook his head. Just nerves.

The one thing he checked the most were the bands holding his blond hair in a ponytail.

He had wound them tight before boarding the helicopter. It wouldn't do for them to snap halfway through the mission. That would be a disaster, an absolute debacle.

His squadmates were lost in their own worlds, their hands performing their own predeployment choreography. They all were ready. Each of the eight men in the copter had completed dozens of lesser runs before transferring to First Response-Alpha Squad. This was the ninth mission they had went on together. Each time set Charles's nerves on edge. Too many variables.

Too much danger.

The overhead whine of the engines changed as the copter came to a hovering stop. The side doors opened and ropes dropped to the ground. One by one, the members of FRAS free rappelled to the ground below. Immediately the squad turned back to back. Charles scanned the area in front of him. All clear so far.

FRAS-Lead, Chet, whispered, "Seven, what's the reading? Better, worse? What are we dealing with here?"

Seven, a young kid named Thompson, held up the sensor pack. "Disruption levels have risen from 10 to 45 while we were en route!"

The squad shifted. A spike meant trouble. Charles's gaze locked on the closest suppression tower. Looked like the blasted thing was working but one could never tell. Obviously something had gone wrong or else FRAS wouldn't be in the field.

"Any idea if it's a Ker or a Ter?" Lead asked.

Seven shook his head. "No clue. Levels are fluctuating. Could be as simple as a few kids hopped up on ley-juice lobbing simple spells. Sensors can misread that. But with the theta levels...might be a bona fide magicker."

Charles glared at the suppression tower. That technology was supposed to keep the magick at bay, but there were ways around it: ley-juice, Arcane-X, or other illegal narcotics could grant a normal human rudimentary casting abilities. FRAS had gone on plenty of runs, ready for a firefight only to discover it was a couple of casters, or "Ters", turning dogs into lizards or setting each other on fire.

But a magicker? The towers were supposed to keep them banished out of the mortal plane. But every now and then, something would go haywire with the field and one could slip into existence and wreak considerable havoc. And there were worse things than magickers that sometimes slipped through...

FRAS was founded fifty years ago to deal with the irruptions of magick which inevitably found their way into civilized society. It had prestige but there were nights when Charles wished the suppression towers worked well enough to put him out of a job.

Like tonight.

Charles barely listened as Lead and Seven argued about where the disturbance might be located. He knew what was coming next. Lead turned to the squad.

"Partner up. Fan out. Locate and capture, fire only if fired upon. Move."

Charles and his partner, Nick (also known as Six), took to the west as the rest of the squad silently fanned out. Charles's breath thundered in his ears as each chirp of a cricket screamed at him. Even the sweet-smelling breeze felt like fire on his exposed skin. The sooner this was over and he was back at the base, the better.

"What do you suppose it is?" Six whispered. "Imp? Goblin? A siren, maybe? Been a while since we've tackled one of them."

Charles ground his teeth together. The last time Six "tackled" a siren, the magicker sued the squad for sexual misconduct. She had no legal standing to bring the suit and got exiled just the same, but clearly Six hadn't learned his lesson.

The muzzle of his gun leapt to each possible hiding place. Chills clawed their way up his throat. A dull ache throbbed around his skull and behind his eyes. He winced. *Not now! Not now!*

A burst of gunfire sliced through the night as someone screamed over the radio, "Delta, delta, del—"

The voice was cut off by a gurgle and a thud. Charles turned to Six, who had paled, his gun trembling in his hand. Code "Delta" was rarely used, an indication of a worst-case scenario. It meant FRAS was grossly out-matched. Tonight's mission wasn't about arresting a Caster. It wasn't about containing a Magicker.

It was confronting a member of an Elder Race, beings bred within and for magick. They were the reason why the suppression towers were built. They were the reason why FRAS carried inhibium-jacketed bullets.

They were also the reason why members of FRAS had short life-expectancies.

"Sounded like Seven," Six speculated. "Let's go."

Charles and Nick jogged southeast in the hopes that Seven and Eight still lived. He tried to calm himself but found it to be a losing battle.

They spotted a fire tucked under an outcropping of rock. Four bodies splayed out around the fire. An old crone stood with her back to them, wrapped in a ratty yet colorful wool blanket, her stringy white hair billowing about her head in a breeze Charles couldn't feel. She sang offkey in a language Charles didn't recognize, yet the words danced like pins across his cheeks and arms. Occasionally, the old woman tossed small brown packages into the fire. The flames burst into different colors and static buzzed in Charles' radio. She turned to face them.

When Charles saw her eyes, he cursed. They were completely black. Worse, the woman floated towards them, her feet hovering six inches above the ground. She was an *iysho*, one of the most powerful Elder races imaginable.

The *iysho* woman cackled, an odd resonance to her voice that rattled Charles's jaw. "So you've come at last, child. I knew it would be you."

Nick raised his weapon and ordered her to surrender. Instead, the crone batted a hand at him and he crumpled. Charles watched him collapse. Nick wore a content smile on his face.

"Don't worry about them," the old *iysho* crooned. "They merely sleep."

Charles stared at the old woman. She floated toward him. She *tsk-tsked* as she moved.

"Metal and plastic and gunpowder, yet nothing you need for what you face," she chided. "This does not bode well, but fear not, I brought a spare."

She rummaged through a pack at her hip. Charles leveled the RD-440 on her. "That's enough! Hands up, back away from the bag."

The crone laughed. "Oh, come now, Charles Logan Tucker. We both know you've never fired a weapon in the field and you certainly won't tonight. Be a good boy and take a seat. You'll need your rest."

Numbness swept Charles's legs out from under him and he dropped. His gaze fixed on the old woman. "How do you know my name?"

"I know much about you. For example, I think it best to give Melissa Benson another call. She's hoping you will ask her out again. You haven't been able to reach her because she's been putting in overtime on a big presentation at the office.

"And your parents, Charles. So proud of you, so thankful for your birth. But the way you treated them, such a shame. The ache? I know about that too. Ma and Da could help you, you know, but instead you ignore them and treat yourself with those nasty chemicals. Not the way to do it. There is such a simpler solution but you fear to try it."

Charles's gaze was drawn to the fire. Images sprang up within the flames. Shady corners, leering faces, money exchanging hands, syringes of bright blue…

He screwed his eyes shut and shook his head but the pictures shimmered in the darkness as if burned there. When he looked, the fire had dimmed and the crone capered around the ring. With each gesture, another part of the fire dimmed.

"No need for it since you are here," she explained. "Enough spell-work to frustrate the towers so you mortals would charge in. But now I have you."

Ice sliced through his skin. What did she mean? She didn't elaborate. Charles pushed himself to his feet and tried to flee. Before he could take three steps, it felt as though his legs had sunk into the ground to his knees. He looked down and much to his horror, that's exactly what happened. He thrashed his legs, hoping to kick them free, but they were stuck fast.

The *iysho* circled him. "Such a mighty warrior, so quick to run. What will happen when the true foe comes?"

"The what?"

"Yes, child. You thought you came out to fight an old woman setting fires in the dark, did you? No, I brought you here to protect your people from the real enemy." She looked off in the darkness. "I can already feel his approach. The towers, they slow him but they cannot stop him. Nothing in your world can. Best get you ready."

From the pack at her hip she drew a small crystalline vial. She waved the bottle under Charles's nose. He was overwhelmed with the aroma: sweet and tangy, filling his sinuses to the point he thought they'd burst. His stomach convulsed even as his mind crashed through a wave of euphoria.

"This is a very rare essence in your world. My family has held onto it for generations out of time for such a day as this. Good we did, yes?"

She poured its contents in front of Charles. At first, it appeared as if the amber liquid soaked right into the earth. Within seconds, though, it flowed out into two channels. The liquid became thicker. It slowly piled into a column that rose a foot from the ground. The woman straightened with a smirk. Charles watched as grooves appeared in the column before him and the liquid hardened into what appeared to be metal.

"Take it," the crone whispered. When he hesitated, she added, "If you don't, you might be trapped like that when he comes and that won't do anyone any good."

Charles looked at her, and when she nodded, he wrapped his fingers around the stub. Hot needles peppered his skin as his hand trembled. Tightening his grip, he pulled, surprised that whatever it was slipped free from its earthen sheath. As he pulled, he realized he too was pulling free from the dirt. He pulled all the harder, his boots and the strange object breaking out of the ground at the same time.

And then he realized he held a glimmering sword.

He dropped it, staring at it with wide eyes. The golden blade flashed as if it produced light of its own, radiating from its double-edged blade down to its gem-encrusted hilt.

The crone *tsk-tsked* again. "Is that the way to treat such a finely crafted weapon? Don't leave it on the ground, boy." She sucked in a nervous breath, her eyes darting around the darkness. "Pick it up! He's here."

The skin on his back puckered. He snatched up his gun and he pointed it toward the park. The darkness deepened and flowed around him. He backed toward the dying embers, thankful for even their dull glow.

"I told you, the weapons of man will be useless against him. Pick up the sword!"

Charles spitted her with an angry gaze then turned his attention to the park. The tingle ricocheted off the base of his skull and raced down his back and into his boots where cold sweat pooled. The crickets had stilled. The park drowned in unearthly silence.

And then reality itself tore to pieces before him.

A glowing crack zigged through the air thirty feet in front of him with a thunderclap that knocked Charles over. Seven's sensor equipment screamed in fury as the crack widened, a creature pushing its way free. Charles glanced at the instruments in Seven's limp hands. The needles had buried themselves at the high end of their spectrum. This wasn't a mere caster. It wasn't a magicker. Even the Elder crone backed away from this monstrosity, whatever it was.

The RD-440 snapped to Charles's shoulder and he fired a round through the portal. Sparks flew as the inhibium tried to dispel the magick, but it didn't work. Scythe-like claws tore at the dirt, trying to gain enough traction to pull itself free. Charles stared as the breach tore wider, revealing a vortex alive with so many colors it hurt his eyes.

Within seconds, the creature emerged from the portal. The living shadow rose to its full height, taller than Charles by several feet. It looked around the park, working its jaws lazily, like a dog licking its lips.

He took a step forward, his gun raised. "By the authority of the United States government, I order you to return from whence you came. Your presence here is in violation of Penal Code Alpha-dash-eight-zero which states all magickal creatures are forbidden to set foot in the mortal realm."

The creature regarded Charles with its cold eyes. A rush of dampness coated Charles from head to toe. It felt as if his body had wrung all of his sweat from itself in one burst. He swallowed hard.

"If you do not comply, I am authorized to use deadly force..."

His voice trailed off as a picture rose within his mind. The dark creature chomped on his broken body before devouring his squadmates for dessert.

Charles shook his head, the vision fading. He glared at the creature. "By the authority of the United States government, I order you to return..."

Another image assaulted his mind. A lithesome blonde stood in a bar surrounded by eager young men. Charles approached the group, calling out her name, yet Melissa Benson ignored him, slicing him with a *sotto voce* comment that caused her admirers to laugh uproariously.

Breath ragged, Charles winced and tried to banish the image from his mind. It was so real! Melissa's laughter echoed in his ears as he brought the RD-440 to his shoulder and fired.

The shot went wide as Charles staggered, a new picture forming in his mind.

This time, he was led from FRAS headquarters in chains. His mind reeled at the thought; they had discovered his secret. He knew agents would soon batter down the doors of Ma and Da's house to arrest them as well. He trudged to the banishment chamber, knowing the intense suppression field would likely shred his body as it forced him out of the mortal plane.

"Child, resist the images!" He could barely hear the crone over his own terrified screams. "You face a fear monger; his weapons are terror and he feeds on your response. Resist him. Fight back!"

Charles steadied himself. The creature's mouth twisted into a rictus of cold pleasure.

Charles frowned, focusing his attention on the spot between the monster's eyes. He fired again, sweat in his eyes as he quelled the rising panic.

The inhibium-jacketed bullets hit home but they passed through the monger's head, sparks trailing their path. The monger winced but then bellowed, a rumbling boom that tore through Charles's chest.

He looked up in time to see the monger charge him and, with one last blast of panic, knocked Charles unconscious.

The first thing he felt was the warmth. Like a blanket tucked securely around his body, it soothed him, calming frayed nerves and washing away the last vestiges of fear.

Charles opened his eyes. He was flat on his back. The *iysho* crone knelt at his side, her fingers dug into his temples. He tried to sit up but she clucked her tongue, refusing to let go.

"Rest, child, rest." She shook her head. "Such a fool, such a fool. I told you mans' weapons wouldn't work and yet you fired anyway. What did you expect to happen? Those fancy metal bits would make the fear monger curtsey and return to the void? Why do you think I made you the sword? Now let me finish the healing."

He closed his eyes. Afterimages of the monger's attacks danced in the darkness. He could feel its hot breath on his chest and stomach as it slowly devoured him. He could smell Melissa's sweet perfume as she cavorted with her admirers. The hum of the banishment chamber thrummed in his ears.

Eventually those memories faded as new strength flooded through his being. The *iysho* crone released his head and Charles sat up, surprised at how good he felt.

"I will give you this: you are much tougher than you appear. Most would curl up in a ball and weep after that strong an attack by the monger. But you, you are ready to fight him again. The question, Charles Tucker, is how will you arm yourself?"

He followed her gaze. His RD-440 rested next to the golden sword. Charles grit his teeth. He didn't look forward to explaining this in his after-action report.

This was crazy. He shouldn't be running around the park in the middle of the night with no back-up and a sword as his only weapon. He shouldn't trust some Delta witch if he was going to face the—what did she call it? Fear monger? He should simply radio back to headquarters and call in Beta Squad.

And yet he couldn't do it. For some reason, his mind was the calmest it had been all night. Charles felt confident, collected, ready for anything. Had the crone enchanted him somehow? No matter. He would face down the monger and dispatch it.

A screech tore through the silence. Tightening his grip on the sword, he sprinted in the direction of the cry.

His stomach lurched at what he found. The monger had doubled in size. It crouched over a young woman, smoky tentacles wrapped around her. Charles crept closer and looked over the victim. While Charles had never seen her before, he was sure she hadn't come into the park with such stunning white hair.

With a savage war cry, he charged the fear monger, sword swinging wildly. The creature turned to face him. A wave of fear coursed through Charles' mind but didn't faze him. It was more like running through a cold ocean wave. The fear monger reared back, releasing its victim as it turned to face him.

Charles skidded to a halt, letting his momentum carry the sword around in what he hoped would be a mortal blow. The sword should have connected, only the fear monger's body rippled away from the blade. The swing almost took Charles off his feet, but he steadied himself and raised the sword between him and the fear monger.

The creature's eyes narrowed at him and another spike of terror grazed his mind. He took a deep breath and closed his eyes and the sensation quickly passed. What was going on? Not long ago, the fear monger paralyzed him in a matter of minutes. Now he could barely prick Charles's mind. What was the difference?

He looked at the sword blazing in his hands with golden light. The monger slunk away from him, snarling, then charged. Its inky tendrils lashed out at Charles.

Charles brought the sword down on the first tentacle. The blade sliced cleanly through the limb. It fell away, dissipating into a gray mist. The monger hissed and pulled back again. A surge of warmth flooded Charles's chest. This was possible. He could beat the monger.

This time he charged. The monger shrank away from Charles as it ducked around trees and bushes. Charles pursued it, herding the creature back...back...

"That's far enough, foul being," a voice said.

Charles looked over the creature's shoulder to see the *iysho* woman behind it. The monger hissed at her. She smiled sadly.

"Such bravery in attacking an unarmed opponent, yet you retreat when faced with a true challenge? I can smell your own fear, beast. Stand and fight or return to the void in shame."

The fear monger hesitated then faced Charles and, with an ear-splitting roar, vaulted. He swung his sword, slicing off another limb, but that didn't stop the monster this time.

Ice wrapped around his arms and legs as the monger drove the flat of the blade to Charles's chest. It enveloped him in a cocoon of shadows. He could feel its chill breath on his neck and cheek. He couldn't move his arms. Wave after wave of fear slapped his mind, each stronger than the last. Horrific images percolated in his mind and soon, Charles knew he would be overwhelmed.

He couldn't let that happen. Anger burned within him as he sucked in a ragged breath. He focused his thoughts on the sword. If he could move it, even a little, maybe...

Much to his surprise, the fear monger's grip slackened. Charles gulped air. He tightened his grip and opened his eyes.

It felt as if he stared into the sun. The sword's brilliant rays hewed through the monger's body. With an agonized scream, the creature fell away, limp. Charles held the sword aloft, its light driving away the darkness and eating more of the monger's body. The foul beast shriveled smaller and smaller.

"Finish it, child," the crone whispered.

Charles brought the sword around and the blade sliced the now tiny monger in two. In a puff of smoke and with a pitiful shriek, the creature vanished into the night air.

Strength drained from Charles's legs. The sword clattered next to him. His mouth was parched and he could smell blood. His? He didn't care.

"Well done, Charles Logan Tucker. I knew you would succeed."

The crone picked up the sword. She caressed the hilt lovingly, then met Charles's gaze. "It served you well, yes? And it is now yours. You never know when you might need it again. But of course, you can't carry this off the field of battle. No, no, too many questions, none of which you would or could answer. So we must sheathe it in a safe place."

Before Charles could react, the woman caught his hair and pulled his head back. His eyes widened as he realized she was dangling the tip of the sword over his right eye. A scream formed in his throat, but the sword melted, the amber liquid pooling over his eye. Warmth rushed down his neck, along his jangled nerves, leaving serenity in its wake. The *iysho* released him and he slumped to his knees, his head lolling forward. She tousled his hair, then cupped his chin in her hand.

"There it will stay, safe and secure until you need it again," she whispered.

With that, she rose and returned to her fire. Charles willed his legs to move. He followed her to the fire ring and watched as she kicked dirt over it. She turned to him.

"Farewell, Charles. May you be well until—"

Her voice turned into an agonized shriek as her body convulsed. She fell to the ground twitching, revealing Six standing behind her, stun gun in hand. He spit on her body.

"Serves you right, you old cow," he said, then looked up at Charles. "Are you okay?"

Charles nodded numbly.

"Good. Let's rouse the rest of the team and get her back to headquarters. I can't wait to banish her and get some sleep."

Fear spiked through Charles as he marched down the hall to the banishment chamber. It was so like the visions he had as he fought the fear monger.

The *iysho* crone's tribunal had been swift and predictable. None of Charles's squadmates had seen the fear monger. The victim from the park couldn't remember the attack. FRAS-Lead didn't believe Charles's story, calling it hallucinations created by Elder magick. Much to Charles's surprise, the crone hadn't said anything either. She stood mute as the governing tribunal ordered her immediate banishment.

As one of her victims, Charles had the right to witness. He didn't want to but felt strangely compelled to be there.

He stepped through the doors into the sterile room housing the banishment chamber. It was a simple box set in concrete, the walls made of true mage-armor, with a suppression field generator wired into its top and floor. Once activated, the generators would force whatever was in the chamber out of the mortal plane. Based on the agonized screams that accompanied the hum of the generators, Charles always suspected it didn't tickle.

He took his place along one wall, the other members of FRAS flanking him. A set of metal doors across the room banged open and the crone shuffled in, her hands shackled with inhibium cuffs. Her guards prodded her into the chamber. She stepped in, her head held high and her eyes shining with pride. One of the guards stepped to the activation switch and turned to her.

"Do you have anything to say?" he asked.

"I do," the crone said.

An uncomfortable murmur rippled through the witnesses.

"Foolish mortals. So desperate to banish the magick from your lives, yet you don't realize how dangerous that is. You assume your technology will keep you safe from what lies beyond this plane, yet you don't realize how vulnerable it truly makes you. None of you can face what waits beyond. Until you realize this, you are all doomed.

"A greater reality strains to break into your world. You are so sure it is nothing but evil that you cut yourself off from what would be a greater good. And you may keep it out for a while, but when the dam breaks, I fear you will all drown." She sighed and her shoulders slumped. "But no matter. Who among you will listen to the words of one old woman? Do what you will. I have said what I can."

The guard threw the switch. The hum of the generators crescendoed to a wail and, in a flash of light, the *iysho* was gone.

After the sentence had been carried out, FRAS-Lead offered to take the squad out for a beer. Charles begged off. He ignored his squadmates persistent efforts to change his mind until they left the barracks.

As Charles left the locker room, Seven called to him from the tech lab. Charles sighed. He wanted to get out of there.

"This'll only take a moment, I swear," Thompson said. He motioned Charles to join him at a monitor. "This was taken when the *iysho* got banished. I thought I saw something unusual during the procedure and wanted to check. Watch this."

On screen, the crone waited in the chamber until, with a flash of light, the generators banished her from the mortal plane. Charles groaned and glared at Thompson. The younger man held up a finger to cut off his words. "Now watch it again in slow motion."

Thompson cued up the footage again. It crawled by, frame by frame. The crone stood stoically, awaiting her fate. Then her face shifted. She looked right into the camera and winked. Then, much to

Charles's surprise, her body faded from view a split second before the generators fired.

"What do you make of that?" Thompson asked. "It appears to me she disappeared before the suppression field could get her."

"I have no idea," Charles finally answered. "Must have been a glitch in the cameras. That happens from time to time due to the suppression fields."

Thompson studied his face for a moment or two then shrugged. Charles patted him on the shoulder before strolling out of the tech lab. He had to restrain himself as he left the barracks. A smile tugged at the corner of his lips. The *iysho* escaped? Normally he would have been horrified at such a development but this time, it didn't really bother him. If anything, he felt relieved. Good for her!

By the time he reached his apartment, the dull ache that accompanied him all evening now threatened to split his head. He wanted nothing more than to deal with the pain and then sleep.

Once he made sure his door was locked, he went into his bathroom and removed the top from his toilet tank. He pulled out a vial which glowed faintly blue in his trembling hand. He grimaced. Almost out. He'd have to hit Little Fairyland soon, see if Ko-Lan had brewed some more Arcane-X.

He twisted the top from the vial, desperate to feel the warmth of the magick ease away his pains. He lifted the vial to his lips.

But then he paused.

Something was different. True, it felt as if his skin would peel from his skull. If he didn't take the Arcane-X, soon people would begin to suspect what he really was. That could lead to uncomfortable questions, possibly jeopardizing his job, his friendships, maybe even his continued existence in the mortal plane.

Yet he didn't care. The gnawing fear that usually dwelt at the back of his mind was silent. It no longer whispered anxiety to him. So what if someone found out? He'd deal with that if it happened.

He held out the vial as far as he could and studied the glimmering contents for a moment, then with a smirk, upended the bottle and dumped the rest into the toilet. He watched with satisfaction as the glowing drug swirled down the drain.

That done, he reached up and undid his ponytail, allowing his hair to break free. As his blond hair spread out into the air, his headache slackened and faded. As his locks swirled around him, practically dancing for joy at its freedom, Charles felt his feet lift off of the bathroom floor. He laughed, the resonance of his voice thrumming through the glass.

He floated there for a moment or two before setting down. There was still one more thing he had to do tonight. He padded into the kitchen and snared the telephone. After dialing the number he had committed to memory weeks earlier, he waited, fighting the urge to hum. Even the humming of a half-*iysho* like himself could wreak havoc on electronics.

"Hello?" a musical voice asked after half a dozen rings.

"Hello, Melissa?" Charles asked, warm confidence surging through his veins. "This is Charles. I was wondering if you were free Thursday night. Say dinner at my place?"

He glanced in a nearby mirror as his wild mane of hair continued to sway in an unfelt breeze and smiled at his own reflection. Maybe tonight wasn't such a bad night after all.

Notes on "Irruption"

This was my second published short story, and it appeared in the now defunct *Dragons, Knights, & Angels* online magazine.

This story was going to be my first foray into a broader world, one in which magic was held at bay by human technology. I had other short stories planned out that would lead into a series of full-scale novels where humans would have to grapple with their decision to banish everything magical from their society. I even tried to write one of the books for NaNoWriMo one year. I made it to the 50,000 word goal, but at that point, I had no idea how to finish the story, so I simply stopped writing and never returned to this storyworld.

But this story is kind of important for another reason. Shortly after *Dragons, Knights, & Angels* bought *Irruption*, they announced they were running a short story contest. They wanted stories that centered around their magazine's name. Each story should feature a dragon, a knight, and an angel. But the publishers issued a challenge: get creative with how you use those prompts. They didn't want to be flooded with retellings of St. George and the Dragon. No, they wanted all sorts of stories, even sci fi!

That intrigued me, so I came up with a story about a freighter captain (my knight) who found a mute girl (the angel) while on a quest to find an alien arifact called "the dragon's heart." I tried writing a short story, but it grew so long that I realized it would make a better book. I decided to participate in NaNoWriMo and tried to adapt this short story idea into a full length novel. Once again, I reached the 50,000 word goal, but this time I had grown to despise all of the characters so badly I stopped writing the novel.

In writing the novel version of *The Dragon's Heart*, though, I came up with an interesting concept: a futuristic version of the Church, one in which all grace has been abandoned. Very legalistic and militaristic, agents for this twisted version of Christianity hunted the freighter captain. I was intrigued by this organization I dubbed "the Ministrix," so much so that after I stopped working on the original novel, I kept thinking about it. Then, while home for Thanksgiving, my family went to see the new James Bond movie, *Casino Royale*, with new-comer Daniel Craig as 007. As I watched Craig take out his enemies, a thought occurred to me: "The Ministrix needs someone like that."

Almost immediately, a man appeared in my imagination, a hulking brute who couldn't feel emotions or pain, someone who killed without remorse in the hopes of saving his soul. He introduced himself to me as "Crusader." And a few days later, I had the outline figured out for my novel, *Numb*.

SATISFACTION GUARANTEED

THE MEMORY EATER SMELLED like it had a bad case of halitosis. Louis gagged and his hands jerked to the helmet's sides to find the seam.

"Hang on, sir, I'll have you out in a moment." The technician's voice was muffled. Strong hands pushed him back into the plush chair.

Louis tried to relax. Within seconds, his eyes watered. The metal walls reflected every bit of heat back into his face. His cheeks felt as though he had laid out in the sun too long. He tried to breathe only through his mouth but soon, his lungs ached. How long did it take to unlock the helmet?

With a hiss, a cool breeze rushed in as the Memory Eater opened. Louis gulped deeply, savoring the fresh air. Bright light stabbed into his eyes. A twinge, the beginning of a headache, twisted behind his eyes. He rubbed the bridge of his nose and the pain evaporated.

A scrawny kid, couldn't have been more than twenty, offered him a paper cup of water. "How do you feel, Mr. Porter?"

"Fine, I think." He tried to still his trembling fingers long enough to take the cup, but he spilled on his khakis. "So we're done?"

"Almost." The technician glanced at a clipboard, tracing whatever was on it with a finger.

Louis took a sip and fought the urge to look at the technician's nametag. His gaze roved over the brown walls, the obviously plastic plants, a painting of a man fishing on a river at sunset. But the bright yellow "TRAINEE" ribbon screamed for his attention. Louis finally gave in and stared at it. His memory wipe had been done by Eric Tipton, Trainee. He tried not to squirm in his chair. Everyone had to start somewhere, but it would have been nice if a supervisor had been watching over the kid's shoulder.

The trainee—Eric—went through a checklist, rattling off symptoms, barely allowing Louis time to answer. No double vision. Yes, he was breathing fine. No, he hadn't "soiled himself" during the procedure. Did that actually happen?

Eric tapped the bottom of the clipboard and looked Louis square in the eye. "Can you tell me why you came to Memory Eater today?"

Louis's mouth popped open but no words came. He frowned, wracking his brain for the answer. Why had he come here? He could remember the advertisements, promising a quick fix to unpleasant memories. He vaguely recalled entering the small clinic and filling out the initial paperwork. But every time he tried to remember what memory he wanted to lose, he couldn't. He stumbled into a pleasant fog.

He finally looked at Eric and shrugged. "I have no idea."

"Excellent." Eric smiled, flashing crooked and stained teeth. He helped Louis out of the chair, patting him on the shoulder. "Then that's it."

"Really?"

"Really. Thank you for coming to Memory Eater, where satisfaction is always guaranteed."

Louis wavered on his feet for a few moments. He had expect-ed...more. Flashing lights, a trumpet fanfare, some grand gesture that would assure him his memory, whatever it had been, was truly gone forever. Instead, Eric gestured for Louis to leave the room.

He nodded to the receptionist on his way out the door. A young couple sat in the lobby, holding each others' hands so tightly their knuckles were white. The girl had been crying. The boy looked mad. For a moment, Louis wondered what brought them to Memory Eater. A fight? A miscarriage? He paused in the doorway for a moment, but a glare from the boy sent him out into the bright sunlight.

As he stumbled to his car, a subtle ache wormed its way between his temples. He grimaced, squeezing the bridge of his nose. Once again, the ache vanished. He slipped behind his wheel and gunned the engine. He couldn't wait to return to his life, free of his painful memory.

Whatever it had been.

When the morning light filtered through his shades, he could scarcely believe it. For the first time in as long as he could remember, Louis had slept through the night. Instead of stumbling into the bathroom for a cold shower to completely wake him up, Louis indulged in a warm shower that invigorated him even more. He actually whistled as he combed his brown hair out of his eyes. And breakfast was something he could enjoy rather than scarf down as he dashed out the door.

As he trotted out to his car, his cell chirped. He glanced at the screen and couldn't help but smile. A text from Melissa, "hope ur day is gr8 c u 2nite <3 u." He flipped the phone open and started a reply.

But as his fingers pecked out his message, his stomach soured, flipping and churning. He didn't want to answer her text. He paused mid-word. What was wrong with him? He hadn't seen Melissa for more than ten minutes for two weeks. But tonight would more than make up for that: the intimate dinner, then a stroll into the park to watch the sunset over the lake, to the one spot he'd picked out for "the question." He'd been anticipating this for weeks now; why would he be so scared?

He shook his head. Nerves, just nerves. Proposing was a big step. As sure as he was, it was only natural that he'd be a little psyched. He finished his reply and pocketed his phone. Plenty of time for nervousness later.

Louis dropped into his chair at B&E Insurance and checked the nearest clock. Five minutes early. He smiled. A good day just kept getting better. He still had no idea why he went to Memory Eater, but clearly, whatever they had removed was for the best. He should have gone months ago.

He tackled his e-mail inbox. Only thirty messages, most inter-office memos regarding tweaks to policies based on market fluctuations. He skipped those, opening the few from salespeople. Most were standard questions about what they did and didn't cover, but one made him chuckle. A customer wanted to know if they'd cover treatments at Memory Eaters.

If only. He started a reply when his neighbor, Grant, poked his head over the cubicle wall.

"Meeting, chief. Pauline's on the warpath."

Louis rolled his eyes. Grant was always convinced that Pauline was upset or angry or out to get him, but their supervisor really wasn't all that bad. Maybe a little rough and distant at times, but he always appreciated her firm hand directing the actuarial department. He scooped up a notebook and fell in step behind Grant for the conference room.

He nodded to the coworkers who had already taken seats, as far from the head of the table as possible. That left him a chair at the midpoint. He opened his notebook, jotted down the date and time of the meeting, and leaned back.

A moment later, Pauline breezed into the room, her arms laden with papers. "Morning, ladies and gentlemen. Sorry to roll you all into here so early, but we've got some new data from the home office that should keep us busy for at least a week."

Two people groaned. Pauline's lips drew taut. Her plush, full lips, so soft and inviting...

Louis blinked and frowned. What was that about?

Pauline started around the table, dropping packets in front of each person. She leaned over the table, revealing a hint of lace that peeked out at him. Her perfume, flowery and sweet, drifted across the table.

And he remembered the last time he smelled it, as she pressed up against him, her fingers raking his back. How those lips, those wet lips, had kissed a fiery trail from his ear to his shoulder. And how his hands sought that lace, roaming...

He gasped as the new data slammed onto the table in front of him. Louis looked up at Pauline. Her features didn't soften, but he thought he caught a glint in her eyes, a hidden smile meant only for him.

"You okay, man?" Grant's whisper sounded as though it traveled down a long tube.

Louis mopped a hand over his face as Pauline stepped past him, her scent stalking him, prompting more memories of frantic whispers in an enclosed space—a closet?—as she pressed against him, both of them trying to keep quiet so they wouldn't get caught. More kisses, her fingers through his hair, then down his back to grab...

With a startled yelp, he pushed himself away from the conference table. He looked around the room at the startled expressions on everyone's faces.

"Is everything all right, Mr. Porter?"

He stared at Pauline. How could she be so stoic, like nothing had happened? She had been so contented afterward, stroking his arm with a lethargic giggle. Then they had dressed, snuck back out to the party, and...

Party? What—

A sharp pain ricocheted through Louis's skull. His hand shot to his temple. "I'm sorry, I'll be right back."

Before Pauline could answer, he darted out of the conference room, ignoring the whispers in his wake.

He tried to walk nonchalantly to the nearest restroom, but he could feel the eyes of his coworkers on him. They knew. They had to. They did their best to ignore him, but their scrutiny chased him until he burst into the empty restroom.

After locking the door, he wrenched on the cold water and splashed some on his face. Several deep breaths, and the headache slowly unwound, taking the panic with it.

What had happened? Slowly the memories came back. Two weeks earlier, there had been a party. The sales team had landed a major account and the folks upstairs deemed it worthy of celebration. The party had started sedately at first, but once the champagne started flowing, people cut loose. He must have had too much and then he and Pauline...

Louis frowned at his reflection in the mirror. Why hadn't he remembered until now? Shouldn't he have remembered when he saw Pauline afterwards? No, wait. She had been on a retreat with the rest of the management staff, just got back yesterday. And he had read once that smells could trigger forgotten memories. So when he caught a whiff of her perfume, it must have pierced whatever wall his drunken mind had built.

The strength drained out of his legs and he almost collapsed. How would he face the department? Or Pauline? Worse, how could he face Melissa tonight, knowing what he had done? It would crush her. It would destroy their relationship.

He couldn't hide in the restroom forever, though. A few more deep breaths, a little more bracing water against his cheeks, and he braved the office again. He tried to keep his head up as he marched back to the conference room and slipped through the door. Pauline glanced in his direction but resumed her presentation. No one else noticed his return. They'd probably gossip about it later.

He tried to focus on what Pauline said, but as she droned on about new statistics and computational models, his mind drifted, more details of their tryst asserting themselves. It wasn't much; most of the encounter was shrouded in a mental fog. But it was enough to drive heat into his cheeks throughout most of the meeting.

After an hour, Pauline dismissed everyone. Before Louis could escape, though, she called, "Hold on a second, Mr. Porter. Can I talk to you for a moment?"

Grant gave Louis a forlorn look. Or was he silently laughing at him? Louis ground his teeth but tried to appear relaxed and unconcerned. As soon as everyone had left, Pauline stepped closer and put a hand on his shoulder. An electric spark zinged through his chest.

"Are you okay?" Her voice, low and husky, drilled straight into his heart. "You're looking a little sick."

Louis swallowed his rising panic. "I'm fine, Pauline. Really." He swallowed again, leaned in a little closer. "And if we could keep what...happened between the two of us, I would really appreciate it."

A look of confusion flitted across her features but she shrugged. "All right, Louis, if that's the way you want it, I guess. Talk to you later."

She breezed out of the conference room. Louis released a slow sigh of relief. At least she was willing to keep it quiet. Now all he had to do was face Melissa.

Tell her, not tell her? The question haunted Louis through the rest of his day and hounded him the whole way home. The more he tried to ignore it, the more persistent it became. Now it dogged his steps as he paced through his apartment.

The intercom blared and Louis nearly jumped out of his skin. He glanced at the clock and winced. Was Melissa here already? His fingers tightened around the velvet box. He had hoped for more time to figure out what he was going to do.

The box buzzed again. He jabbed the switch, hoping it'd turn out to be Mormon missionaries. "Yes?"

"Hey, sweetie, can you buzz me in?"

Of course it wasn't. He banged his head against the doorframe and stabbed the button.

"Thanks! I'll be up in a second."

Louis launched himself away from the door and resumed his pacing through his tiny living room. He tossed the ring box between his hands. He had to figure out what he was going to do and fast.

His gaze fell on the rickety table in his kitchen. Sure, the checkered table cloth was stained and a bit of a cliché, and the candles didn't really match. But the corner glowed, warm and inviting. And while Louis didn't consider himself even a decent cook, the smells wafting through the apartment were right too. Melissa's favorite meal simmered on the stove top, a pork cider stew. Maybe that wasn't "traditionally romantic," but it was the first meal he cooked for her. Nostalgia alone dictated he make it tonight. Everything would have been perfect...

If he hadn't remembered what happened with Pauline.

He shoved the ring into his pocket. Why did he have to remember today? No, why did he sleep with Pauline in the first place? He had a good thing with Melissa. He had known it from their second date. And now, thanks to his stupidity, he had wrecked everything.

Maybe he didn't have to tell her. A smile tugged at his lips and his fingers curled around the box in his pocket. Pauline wouldn't say anything, right? She liked Melissa. They had always gotten along at company get-togethers. And Pauline would probably get in trouble, seeing as she was his supervisor. So yeah, there was really no reason for Melissa to find out. He should propose and forget anything ever happened. He could even go back to Memory Eater and wipe it out.

His stomach sunk. No, that was no good. Even if he no longer remembered it, Pauline would and there was no guarantee that she wouldn't talk about it. If anyone at the office knew, they could say something too. As much as he didn't want to, he'd have to tell Melissa. He glanced at the table again. What had been intended to be a romantic engagement dinner would hopefully soften the blow.

He chewed on his bottom lip. She wasn't going to like this. The last thing in the world he wanted to do was disappoint her. Not again, not especially since that night...

Louis frowned as the memory washed over him. He had wanted to go for a ride out in the country to see the stars. She drove, insisted on going too fast. A dark shape darted out into the road. Melissa didn't brake, only laughed as whatever it was thumped against the car. The next day, Louis saw a report about a child killed in a hit-and-run along that same country road. He told Melissa he was going to go to the police. She hadn't said anything, not at first, but then she cracked her knuckles and said that if he did, she would be very "disappointed." And her tone carried the threat very well.

Louis blinked and shook his head. His girlfriend was a killer. How could he have forgotten about that? Had he repressed the memory?

A steel spike slammed through his temple, setting his brain on fire. He clutched at his head and stumbled into a nearby wall. A ragged gasp burst up his throat.

The apartment door burst open and Melissa breezed in. Her long red hair was pulled into a tight ponytail, her brown eyes bright. As he had requested, she wore the tight black dress that accentuated her every curve. Her cheery smile faltered when she saw him. She dropped her purse and rushed to his side.

"Baby? Are you okay? What's the matter with you?"

Her words slammed into him. She had asked the same thing when he freaked out in the car. *What's the matter with you?* Like hitting someone on a darkened road was no big deal!

With a moan, he slid down the wall and curled into a tight ball as agony ricocheted through his skull. Melissa wrapped her arms around him, rubbing his arms and chest.

Her bloody hands, hands that had clutched the wheel while she laughed and murdered an innocent little girl...

Louis yanked free of her grasp. "Get away from me!"

Melissa's eyes widened. "Louis, what are you—"

He scrabbled away from her. "I remember what you did. All of it."

She frowned. "And what did I do?"

How dare she look confused! Why had he stayed with her? How could he have ever considered proposing to a monster like her?

Melissa smiled and reached out a hand. "Look, why don't you settle down? Take a few deep breaths and then we can maybe eat some dinner? I've been looking forward to seeing you all day. Please?"

He hesitated. She seemed so sincere, so earnest. But he couldn't rid himself of the feeling of the car bouncing, of the sickening thud that echoed through the floor.

"You need to go." His words were a hoarse whisper. "Now."

Her lip trembled but she nodded. "All right."

He buried his head in his arms as she backed out of the apartment.

The smell of pork cider stew clung in the air, mocking him.

Louis groaned and rolled over on the couch. The clock on his VCR said it was close to midnight. The thundering agony in his head had slithered away an hour earlier, leaving behind a dull ache radiating down his neck and into his shoulders. The blue velvet box that held Melissa's engagement ring glared at him from the coffee table. Tonight was supposed to be perfect. Now he had another memory to purge. Memory Eaters was going to get rich off of him.

He levered himself up and ran his fingers through sweat-soaked hair. He should call Melissa, but then she'd only want to come over and he wasn't sure he could face her again so soon. Maybe the best thing to do would be to get some sleep, call her tomorrow night.

As he staggered for his bedroom, the apartment door rattled. Someone was trying to open it. Ice shot up his spine. Had Melissa come back? Maybe she had come to silence him.

The rattling stopped, only to be replaced by insistent pounding. A woman shouted his name. Who could that be? He crept to the door and peeked through the hole.

Only to see a ghost.

His mother's face filled his view. But that was impossible. His mother was dead.

"Son, open up! Melissa called me and we're both very worried. Are you okay?"

Melissa had talked to her? How was that possible? He had been at the funeral when he was six. He remembered trudging through ankle-deep snow to the gravesite, huddling against his father for warmth as the priest said the words and made all the gestures. She had been gone for so long, how could she be standing outside his apartment door?

Fire slashed through his skull, bright sparks exploding in his vision. He pitched forward, catching himself against the wall as an electrical storm raged behind his eyes. His "mother" kept talking, demanding he say something or she'd call the police.

"No...no." He swallowed and found his voice. "I'm okay. Really."

There was a long pause. "Are you sure?"

"Yeah...uh, Mom. I am. Just had a rough night is all. I'm okay now, though. Really." What could he say to get rid of her? "I'll call you later?"

Another pause. "Open the door, Louis. I'm not leaving until I see your face."

Louis stared at the door. She wanted— No, not going to happen. He didn't want to face whatever it was impersonating his mother.

She pounded on the door. If she wasn't going to leave...

He opened the door, keeping the security chain on.

The woman certainly looked like his mother, or at least, how she might have looked if she had lived to be that old. She frowned at him in such a familiar way, that he—

A knife stabbed into his forehead, twisting slowly. He gasped and doubled over, clutching at his temples.

"Sweetheart, are you all right?" His mother tried to press through the opening.

"I'm just...coming down with a cold." He seized on that lie. "And I don't want you to catch it. Melissa either; that's why I sent her home. Just please, go."

Her lips pursed together for a moment. "All right, if that's what you want. Just call me later, okay?"

As if he had her number...or did he? Another blade of pain drove deep into his brain, setting his skull on fire.

When he looked up again, she had gone. He took several ragged breaths and stumbled to his bedroom.

What was happening to him? Why were so many memories surfacing now?

His gaze fell on a brochure from Memory Eater. Had they done something to him? Maybe erasing that memory, whatever it was, dislodged these painful ones. He snatched up the trifold paper and looked over the fine print. Nothing in there about headaches or recovering suppressed memories. But this had to be it. What else could it be?

Louis tumbled onto his bed without bothering to strip out of his clothes. The sooner he got to sleep, the better. He suspected he'd have a long day tomorrow.

Calling in sick the next day had been more challenging than he planned. Pauline had answered. Her voice caused his stomach to lurch as he made his excuse. She, of course, was perfectly understanding, wishing him a speedy recovery.

As soon as he was off the phone with her, he drove down to Memory Eater. Whereas two days earlier, the clinic appeared happy and cheerful, Louis couldn't help but shudder as he walked through the glass doors.

The receptionist looked up and smiled as he walked through the doors. "Back already? You know, sir, we usually recommend people wait at least a week between treatments."

He shook his head. "I need to talk to your manager."

Her smile froze. "Is there a problem, sir?"

"I think you guys messed up my brain somehow."

Without taking her eyes off of him, she punched in a few numbers into her phone and whispered into her headset. Her smile widened, but it didn't reach her eyes. "Mr. Isley will be with you in a few moments."

Louis wandered around the lobby, cataloging the out-of-date magazines, the painting of a lighthouse in the middle of a storm, the sickly plant straining for the only window. He winced as another pain wormed through his forehead. Was he about to remember something horrible that happened in this office? Thankfully, the pain disappeared just as quickly as it appeared.

"Mr. Porter?" A portly man in his fifties, wearing a rumpled shirt and tie, stepped out of the back. According to the ID on the man's lanyard, his name was Steven Isley, a senior manager for Memory Eater. "Come this way, please."

Isley led Louis through the doors and into a cramped office, one with bare white walls and a tiny window that allowed only a meager amount of light in from the outside. Isley sucked in his gut as he slunk around the battered desk that filled most of the room.

"So what seems to be the problem?" Isley asked.

"I came in yesterday to have a memory erased and since then, I've been remembering all sorts of horrible things." Louis went on to explain about Pauline, Melissa, and his mother.

Haflway through the story, Isley frowned and started typing on his computer. The chirps and beeps sounded like an instant messaging program. Heat flashed up Louis's spine. The least Isley could do was give him his full attention.

As Louis wrapped up his tale, Isley glanced up at him. "You were in yesterday? And Eric was your technician?"

Louis nodded. Isley groaned.

"Well, that explains a lot. Let's take a walk, okay?"

The supervisor led him through the halls and into the room with the Memory Eater machine. Louis hung back in the door, regarding the metal helmet like some sort of dangerous animal. Isley laughed.

"It's okay, Mr. Porter, I just want to show you something." He beckoned him to step closer to the device.

With a shaky breath, Louis took a step into the room. Isley turned to the wall, opening up a panel to reveal a number of cylinders, blinking lights, and wires.

"Everyone thinks that a Memory Eater just wipes out a memory, like an eraser on a white board. It's not nearly that simple. You've got to access the brain via the hippocampus and look for the different threads of the memory through the various nooks and crannies. The technician then extracts the memory and deposits it here." He pointed to a small black box, one lined with blinking blue and green lights. "The Memory Eater then breaks down the memory further and flushes it from the system.

"Problem is, little bits of data get stuck. Over time, those bits build up. A technician needs to purge the system once a day. If the technician doesn't, the flotsam can build up and eventually, the system will...well, regurgitate it into someone."

Louis stared at the component. "The Memory Eater puked into my brain?"

Isley shrugged. "I suppose that's one way of looking at it."

"So those memories..."

"Were leftovers from other people. You never slept with your boss, your girlfriend didn't kill anyone, and offhand, I'd say you didn't really attend your mother's funeral."

Louis gaped at the supervisor for a moment. "But if they were other people's memories, why did I remember Pauline and Melissa and—"

Isley waved away his question. "You didn't get the full memories, just bits and pieces, a suggestion: 'I slept with my boss' or 'My significant other murdered someone.' Your mind filled in the blanks. That's probably why you were getting the headaches. Extreme cognitive dissonance. Part of you is sure it happened, another part knows it didn't, they have a tug of war and your brain is the rope."

Why was Isley so nonchalant about this? And how did he know that's what happened? Unless... "You're saying this has happened before?"

The other man nodded. "Sure. Lots of times. Purging the system isn't SOP. It's a glitch we've discovered since this version of the device was released. Don't worry, I'll have a talk with Eric and we've notified corporate. Hopefully they'll revise the manual."

Louis's mind groped for the right words. He stammered for a moment and paced in a tight circle before he whirled on Isley. "Do you realize what I've been through? The sheer hell I experienced yesterday?"

"Oh, I'm sure." Isley tucked his hands into his pockets. "Just be thankful you figured out what was happening now. One time, we had a lady who didn't come in for six months. By the time she came to see us again, she was a gibbering mess. Boy, was her husband steamed."

How could Isley be so cavalier about all of this? "You don't seem all that concerned about any of this. Aren't you worried I'm going to sue you?"

Isley shrugged. "Not particularly, no."

Pain pricked Louis's shoulder. He whirled around, surprised to see the receptionist holding a hypodermic needle. Warm metal coursed down his neck and into his arms and legs, dragging him down to the floor. Darkness swirled in his vision and he fell into the void.

As Louis's eyes fluttered open, the Memory Eater's rancid smell clawed at his nose. He gagged, his hands jerking to the helmet's sides, trying to find the seam and pull it free.

"Hold on, Mr. Porter, I'll have you out in a jiff." The technician's voice was muffled, but a strong hand pushed Louis's chest, holding him in the plush chair.

With a hiss, the helmet opened and cool air rushed in. Louis gulped deeply. Relaxation dribbled through Louis, pooling in his chest.

A portly man in a rumpled shirt and tie held out a paper cup of water. "How do you feel, Mr. Porter?"

"Great." He waved away the drink. "So we're done?"

"Almost." The man, whose lanyard identified him as "Steven Isley," launched into what sounded like a memorized list of symptoms.

Louis answered each question. No double vision. Yes, he was breathing fine. No, he hadn't "soiled himself" during the procedure. Did that actually happen?

Isley smiled warmly. "Can you tell me why you came to Memory Eater today?"

Louis's mouth popped open but no words came. He frowned, wracking his brain for the answer. Why had he come here? He vaguely recalled the car ride over. He was upset about...something. But every time he tried to remember what, he couldn't. He stumbled into a pleasant fog.

He finally looked at Isley and shrugged. "I have no idea."

"Excellent." Isley helped Louis out of the chair. "Then that's it."

"Really?"

"Really." Isley motioned for Louis to leave the room, gently moving him along with a hand on his back. "Thank you for coming to Memory Eater, where satisfaction is always guaranteed."

Notes on "Satisfaction Guaranteed"

So I SPEND WAY too much time on Kickstarter. When I ran my first campaign there, someone commented on the sheer number of projects I've backed over the years. I'm particularly addicted to boardgames, but occasionally, I'll dip my toe into supporting a publishing project or two.

That's how I found out about a short story anthology called *The Memory Eater*. The concept was simple: suppose there was a machine that could erase a person's memory. How would that affect society? I not only backed the project, I also decided to write this story about how such a product might glitch and cause problems for those who use it. But I also realized that, given the technology's existence, it could also be used to make sure that everyone loved it without reservation.

I don't know how much the editor liked my story, but it was the second story in the anthology. No idea if that means anything.

THE NIGHT QUEEN

"Don't botch this up, kid." Captain Richardson's hot breath stung Josiah's ear. "You want to earn your share? You make sure your readings are solid, got it?"

Josiah tried to ignore the captain's looming presence. The man's breath alone was overpowering, a sickly mix of eggs and coleslaw. His constant need to badger Josiah didn't help. For a fleeting moment, Josiah wished he could elbow the old man in the gut to get him to back off.

"C'mon, Cap, ease up. You keep ridin' him that hard, he's liable to piss himself." Thompson, the demolitions expert, didn't look up from sharpening a knife that stretched the length of his forearm.

"We don't have room for error on this." Richardson smacked the back of Josiah's chair. "Do you know how much I paid to get this lead? We won't have an opportunity like this again. That's for certain."

Thompson snorted. "We ain't got much of an opportunity now. Right, kid?"

Josiah swallowed a groan and squeezed the bridge of his nose. He had never imagined a salvage run would be like this. The tri-vids at home had made it seem so glamorous: find derelict spacecraft, strip them for valuables, and sell to the highest bidder. Money, girls, adventure—everything Josiah ever wanted—would finally be in his grasp. It'd be better than working at the family aquaponic farm the way Dad wanted him to. He figured there'd be more money in wrecked ships than tilapia. So he'd gone to the nearest port, lied about his age, and shipped with the first captain to sign him. Now he was trapped in a contract with an abusive jerk. Josiah wished he could go back in time two months and slap some sense into his younger self.

Apparently Richardson wanted to help with the slapping part. Sharp pain flashed through the back of Josiah's skull. "Keep your eyes on the sensors, boy! I'm not paying you to daydream!"

As if the captain would pay him. So far Josiah had helped salvage two tugs and an empty freighter, but Richardson had claimed Josiah's share as "training and boarding expenses." Josiah would probably wind up in debt to the captain by the time his contract was up.

"As ordered." Josiah forced the words through his clenched teeth. "What am I looking for again?"

"You'll know it when you see it." Richardson stomped over to the astrogation panel. "Arrival in five seconds. Look sharp, Thompson."

Thompson tossed his knife end over end and then snatched it out of the air. "Always, Cap."

A tremor wormed through the deck beneath Josiah and the constant droning of the engines grew quiet, more sedate. Josiah leaned over the sensor readouts.

Once again, Richardson loomed behind him. "Well? What do you see?"

Josiah bit his lip, not wanting to answer honestly. The captain sounded so eager, so sure of himself, that Josiah wished he could say he saw something of interest. But no, all that was out there was a gas giant, with a small flock of three dozen orbiting moons, and—

Wait? What was that?

At first, it looked like nothing more than a sensor ghost in the planet's rings. But once Josiah had focused on the object, more details emerged. A large mass of heavy metals, much larger than the salvage vessel. What's more, the sensors detected the intermittent signal of an engine core, erratic but functional. A ship? If so, it was huge, large enough to carry thousands of people.

Josiah shook his head. Best not to keep the captain waiting. "I've got something."

Richardson sucked in a sharp breath. "ID?"

"Working on it." Josiah's slender fingers danced over the sensor controls. An image of the other vessel appeared on screen, a stately and sleek starliner with wide, glassed-in viewing galleries. Six engine bells flared from the stern.

Josiah frowned. He had seen images of this ship before, but he couldn't quite place it. He focused the visual sensors on the bow. Brilliant red letters stood out against the pristine white hull.

Ice sluiced through Josiah's veins. No way. It couldn't be.

"Yes?" Richardson's voice had dropped to a bare hiss.

"It's the *Night Queen.*"

Thompson's knife clattered to the deck. Josiah couldn't blame him. Even though it had disappeared thirty-five years earlier, long before Josiah had been born, he knew the details. Launched from the Orion colonies, the *Night Queen* had carried 4,000 passengers, some of the wealthiest people in the galaxy, on a maiden voyage that ended when the ship vanished. He never imagined he'd be the one to find the lost starliner. Suddenly his dreams of quick wealth seemed like a distinct possibility.

"Excellent." Richardson's voice brimmed with excitement.

Thompson retrieved his knife from the floor and slipped it into a sheath at his hip. "Forgive me for saying it, Cap, but you don't seem all that surprised. You knew she was out here?"

"Sort of. A Federate survey mission passed through here a month ago. One of the techs spotted the wreck but didn't get a good reading. He sold me the data, and it looked right. I figured it was worth a shot."

Thompson's expression soured. "If the Federates know about this..."

Richardson shook his head. "Let's just say I made sure the tech is willing to remain discreet. We've got a week before he'll report his findings, more than enough time to strip her to the hull."

Thompson's lips peeled back into a predatory grin.

Josiah shifted in his seat, glancing at the readings again. "Don't you think the passengers' families deserve to know what happened to their loved ones?"

The captain shrugged. "We'll inform them, but only after we've seen what's on board. Keep scanning. Leave the details to us."

Josiah turned back to the sensors, stung. He tried to focus on the readings spooling by on the readout. And yet he couldn't stop thinking about the dead onboard and those mourning them.

Three hours later, Josiah had scanned the entirety of the *Night Queen*, leaving him with too many unanswered questions.

"You done yet, boy?" Richardson asked.

The answer caught in Josiah's throat. He didn't want to share what he had found: that the *Night Queen* was in pristine condition. No hull breaches, the engines hadn't overloaded, and all of the escape pods seemed to be in place. The paint hadn't even been chipped by micrometeorite collisions. The *Night Queen* appeared as if she had just left dry dock brand new. Even the engines were still on-line, powering the ship.

It made no sense. If everything was intact, why had she disappeared? More puzzling, if she had been in orbit of this gas giant for the last three decades, why hadn't she sustained any damage? Needles of ice danced over his skin as he tried to decipher the mystery.

Captain Richardson, however, wasn't willing to wait. He shoved Josiah out of the way and leaned over the sensors. He hooted and pounded the console with his fist. "Excellent! If the interior is intact as well, we should get a good haul." The captain dropped into the pilot's seat, and his stubby fingers stabbed at the controls. "Let's dock and see what we can find."

A slight tremor in the deckplates tickled Josiah's feet. He frowned. Something felt off. Yes, the engines tended to rattle the ship, but that faded quickly. This time, the tremor turned to a shudder, then to shaking, then to a rocking that nearly pitched Josiah out of his seat.

"What's going on?" Richardson demanded. His fingers clawed at the piloting station, his knuckles white.

Josiah couldn't answer. His teeth ground together as the violent bucking intensified. The entire ship howled around him, starting as a low moaning that pitched higher and higher until a deafening shriek swirled through the bridge.

And then a voice, low and grating, the sound of massive rocks grinding together deep within a planetary core, spoke: "Leave us. You are not welcome."

"Says who?" Richardson shouted.

The voice repeated its message, so loudly that Josiah clapped his hands over his ears. If this kept up, the ship would shake itself to pieces. In mere seconds, he would be sucked out into the vacuum, taking up orbit with the *Night Queen* around the planet. He laughed, a mirthless bark. He didn't even know the gas giant's name.

Silence sliced through the cacophony. The violent shimmy stopped. Josiah still clung to the edge of his chair, expecting it to start again.

After a few moments of tense peace, Richardson hauled himself out of the pilot's chair. He turned to Thompson and jabbed a finger at him. "Go check the ship, make sure we're not venting atmosphere or anything." As soon as Thompson disappeared from the bridge, the captain whirled on Josiah. "What did you miss?"

Josiah glanced between the sensor console and the captain. "Nothing! There were some anomalies, sure, but there was nothing that would—"

Richardson yanked Josiah out of his chair and leaned over the sensor console. He scowled at the data readout for a few moments before snorting. "Thought so. What's that, genius?"

Josiah peeked over the captain's shoulder. A faint ion trail, probably caused by the engines of another ship, twisted through the system, heading for the *Night Queen*.

"From a Federate ship?" A guess, but Josiah hoped he was right.

Richardson shook his head. "No way. The fuel mix is all wrong for the Federates. No, I've seen this signature before. It's..." The captain's eyes narrowed to dangerous slits. "Sanchez."

Josiah's eyes widened. He had never met Sanchez, but the captain had spoken of her often enough. Richardson's former partner, she'd stabbed him in the back six years ago, cutting him out of the best salvage operation they'd ever run. Since then, she was always one step ahead of Richardson, claimed the best salvage and leaving him the crumbs.

The big man's hands spasmed into fists. "Thompson! We gotta move! If she thinks a little shake and shimmy is going to scare me off..."

"You think she did that?" The question escaped Josiah before he could think about it.

"Isn't it obvious? She hasn't been able to start a salvage operation yet. So she set up something to scare off the competition. We have to move fast, get in there and claim the wreck before she can return. Thompson!"

"Way ahead of you, Cap." Thompson handed Richardson a holstered weapon. "Ship is good. Whatever that was knocked some cans out of the galley cupboards, that's about all."

"Good." Richardson strapped on the gunbelt. "Let's get what's ours."

Josiah eyed the captain's gunbelt. Shouldn't he be armed too?

Thompson patted him on the shoulder. "Don't worry, kid. If you get scared, you can always hide behind me. I'll protect you."

Somehow Josiah didn't find that reassuring.

A rhythmic clanking echoed through the ship as the salvage vessel docked with the *Night Queen*. Josiah jumped, the muscles in his arms twisting painfully tight. Would they hear another angry command, ordering them to leave? When nothing happened, he relaxed, but only a little. His stomach tumbled at the thought of boarding the derelict.

Richardson slapped the back of Josiah's head again. "No day-dreaming, boy. Get on the probe controls and see what we have."

Josiah rubbed his head to massage away the sharp sting. Ever since he discovered the ion trail, Richardson had been a coiled spring. If they didn't get on board the *Night Queen* soon, Josiah worried the captain would snap.

Josiah slipped through the narrow corridor and into the expansive cargo bay. He hesitated in the door for a moment, the deep shadows pressing down around him. A chill shimmied up his spine, radiating out through his arms. But he couldn't keep the captain waiting. A quick jog through the emptiness took him to the airlock hatch.

The probe, little more than a box on wheels, squatted next to the hatch. Josiah pulled on the virtual reality helmet and slipped on the control gloves. After Josiah switched on the system, a hologram sprang to life inside the helmet, hovering before his face, an image of what the probe could "see" through its sensor. The airlock hatch towered over him, his own dark shadow looming across the pitted metal. Weaving his hand through the proper motions, Josiah ordered the hatch open and the probe rolled through.

"We haven't got all day, boy! What are you waiting for?" Richardson's voice, though tinny through the helmet speakers, still carried enough venom to cause Josiah to wince.

"Equalizing pressure now," Josiah reported.

A hiss shot past the probe, and the doors to the *Night Queen* ground open. Josiah swallowed as a well-lit but empty hallway appeared before him. He ordered the probe forward but it hesitated, as if it didn't want to enter the derelict alone. Josiah revved its engine and finally, it darted forward.

The probe skittered down the corridor, and Josiah swiveled its sensors left and right. The interior matched the exterior: the walls gleamed, the carpet looked untouched, and according to the atmospheric readings, the life support systems were still working. But beneath the virtual reality helmet, Josiah frowned. It all looked too perfect. Where had the passengers gone? The probe rolled by a corner lounge, the furniture, the decor, all in place, as if waiting for human occupancy.

Five minutes crept by and the probe moved deeper into the *Night Queen*. By Josiah's count, he had passed sixteen cabins and an entrance to a promenade but he still hadn't found any indication the *Night Queen* had ever been occupied. Had the passengers abandoned this part of the ship after the disaster? But if that were the case, why would they have cleaned up after themselves so thoroughly?

The probe rolled past a bank of escape pods, still in their berths. So the passengers hadn't abandoned ship. Josiah grunted. That would have explained a lot, but—

Josiah paused the probe to get a better look at the control bank. The whir of the probe's engines died, only to be replaced by the sound of footsteps behind him.

Josiah turned, lifting the helmet up to peek into the shadowed cargo bay. Nothing. And yet, he could still hear the footfalls, coming closer...

No, wait. *He* wasn't hearing footsteps. The probe was!

He tugged the helmet in place and frantically signaled for the probe to turn around. The wheels dug into the carpet, and the probe spun in place, even as the footsteps sounded louder and louder in the helmet. Josiah trained the sensors on the hallway behind the probe.

Nothing.

Josiah's breath thundered in his ears, filling the helmet. His heart ricocheted off his ribs. He squinted at the holographic images. Tense minutes unraveled until Josiah calmed himself. He shook his head. He must have imagined the whole thing. Taking several deep breaths to steady himself, Josiah ordered the probe to turn around. The wheels hummed, and the images inside the helmet spun...

Only to come to rest on a small boy staring at the probe with wide eyes.

Josiah gasped. Whoever the boy was, he looked horrible. His clothing was little more than rags, his blond hair ratty and matted. His eyes, blue pools, shone in the bright light, his lower lip trembling. He spun and dashed down the corridor, disappearing around a corner.

"Hey, wait!" Josiah cried, then snarled at his own stupidity. The boy couldn't hear him. He ordered the probe forward. It careened down the hall, almost tipping over as it shot around the corner—

A brilliant flash of light sliced through Josiah's eyes, accompanied by a loud shriek. He ripped off the helmet and tossed it onto the floor. He stared at it for a few moments, then cautiously picked it up and peeked inside. The holographic interface had gone dark, the signal from the probe lost. He looked up at the sealed airlock door, his breath ragged.

"What's going on down here?" Richardson stomped through the cargo bay, Thompson in his wake.

Josiah glanced down at the helmet, then up at the captain. "I think...I think something destroyed the probe."

Richardson's face screwed up into a scowl. "What did you do?"

"Nothing! I heard footsteps, and then there was this little kid, but when I tried to catch up with him, a light flashed and—"

The captain glanced at Thompson, who rolled his eyes with a chuckle.

"Kid's just jumpy is all, Cap. Cut him some slack."

Heat flashed through Josiah. "I am not!"

Richardson slammed into Josiah, driving him up against the bulk-head. Josiah squirmed under the captain's iron grip, but Richardson pressed a forearm against Josiah's throat.

"Do you know what's on that ship? Rare art by the Geoshan master Kirkwall. Uncut Orion gems. Twenty crates of six-hundred-year-old brandy from Earth Prime. And that's just in the cargo holds. No telling how much wealth is waiting for us just beyond that airlock. I'm not gonna let some vac-head, waste-of-atmosphere like you ruin this for me, got it? Now suck it up and let's get going."

"But the probe—"

"It's Sanchez! She must have rigged a trap and you rolled the probe right into it."

"But—"

"Shut up! You'd better keep it together, got it?"

Josiah didn't meet the captain's wild gaze. Richardson snarled and pressed harder. Josiah winced but nodded. Richardson stepped back, allowing him to slide to the deck.

"I'm docking the cost of that probe from your cut."

Richardson stepped over him into the airlock. Thompson started to follow, but he paused, stretching out his hand to help Josiah up. Josiah grabbed hold and started to pull himself up, but Thompson let go. Josiah fell with a thud.

The demolitions expert laughed. "Keep up, kid. You wouldn't want the spooks to get you too."

Thompson disappeared into the airlock. Josiah followed rubbing his rear. As soon as he got his cut, no matter how big it was, he was out of here. He just hoped he survived long enough to collect it.

"Deploying lock-pick." Thompson pressed a small lump of explosives against the cabin door, jamming a detonator into the gray goo and taking a step back.

Josiah rolled his eyes. Was Thompson going to make that dumb joke for every cabin?

With a muffled *whump*, the explosive blew a hole in the door. Thompson stuck his hands into the opening and forced the doors open. Richardson brushed past him into cabin beyond. Thompson glanced at Josiah and made a grand, sweeping gesture with his arms as if welcoming him to high tea.

Richardson wasted no time. He pulled the drawers from their slots and dumped them on the floor. He ripped the sheets from the bed and looked underneath. With a roar, he tipped over a bedside stand and kicked it across the room. "Where is everything? Every cabin, empty!"

Josiah looked away, not wanting to anger the captain further. By his count, they had ransacked a dozen cabins and found nothing. The beds were made, the lights on. They looked like images from an advertising brochure. But they hadn't found any luggage or any indication anyone had ever been in them.

Thompson leaned against the open doorframe, idly picking at his fingernails. "Maybe this part of the ship wasn't used?"

Richardson shook his head. "According to the records, the ship was booked full. No empty rooms. I don't get it."

Josiah glanced over Thompson's shoulder to the corridor beyond. He wanted nothing more than to leave the *Night Queen*, the planet, the entire system behind and look for something else.

"Let's move on. Next cabin." Richardson dusted off his hands.

Thompson saluted, smirking. "Got it, Cap."

Josiah sighed, nudging one of the overturned drawers with his toe.

"You have something to say, boy?"

He didn't meet the captain's gaze. "No, sir."

"I think you do. You've done nothing but sulk since we came on board. If you have an opinion, some insight into what we should be doing, now's the time to share it."

Josiah shrugged. "No, it's nothing. I just—"

Thompson bellowed from the hallway, an indistinct shout that suddenly bled into a blood-curdling scream. Richardson shoved past Josiah into the corridor. Josiah hesitated for a moment, casting one last look around the trashed cabin, and then followed the captain into the hall.

Richardson stood in front of a cabin door, staring at the explosives packed along the lock. But Thompson was nowhere to be seen. Instead, a detonator and his knife lay on the deck as if dropped. Josiah turned a full circle, looking for some sign of struggle, maybe scuff marks on the carpet. Nothing. The demolitions expert had simply vanished.

The captain picked up the knife and stared at the blade. Large chunks of the black metal were gone, as if melted away. Wisps of smoke curled from the blade. Richardson glanced at Josiah. His eyes grew wide and he ripped the gun from his holster, aiming the weapon at Josiah.

Josiah threw up his hands. "What are you doing?"

"Behind you."

Josiah whirled and found the young boy staring up at him with his wide eyes. How had the kid snuck up on them like that? Did he have something to do with Thompson's disappearance?

Richardson stomped forward, his eyes alight with fury. "Where's Thompson? What did you do to him?"

The boy took a step backwards, as if getting ready to run. A crimson laser blast burned through the carpet at his feet.

"Don't you move!" Richardson roared. "You're not going any-where until I find out—"

Josiah stepped between the captain and the boy, knocking the gun away. "What is the matter with you?"

Richardson snarled and tried to side-step him. Josiah moved, spreading out his arms to block his way.

"I'm not going to let you hurt him," Josiah said. "Dock my part of the haul, if you have to, but can't you see that he's scared? He's only a kid."

For a moment, Richardson's features softened. He looked down at the gun, which dipped lower.

"I'm just as worried about Thompson." Josiah wasn't lying, not really. "But this isn't the way."

Richardson nodded. He holstered his gun and slowly stepped around Josiah. "I'm sorry, kid. I'm just worried about my partner, and—"

Josiah turned. The boy had vanished once again. Richardson stared at the carpet. Even the burn mark from the laser had disappeared.

"Sanchez!" The captain spit the word like a curse. With an inartic-ulate roar, he stabbed the knife into the wall. The blade ricocheted off and clattered to the floor. "Where are you?"

The captain stormed off. Josiah jogged after him, not sure why he was following Richardson but not wanting to be left alone either.

They ran deeper into the ship, past shut cabin doors, a pristine dining room, the still full swimming pool. Josiah catalogued it all as he ran. He didn't like it. They still hadn't found a single sign of the original passengers, the probe, the little boy, or Thompson. Worse, a heavy dread pressed down on him, as if the corridor walls were collapsing.

Richardson bellowed Sanchez's name, pausing only long enough to look in open rooms for his nemesis. He skidded to a halt in an open atrium.

A massive tree filled the open space, branches straining toward a clear dome. Beyond the dome, the swirling clouds of the gas giant danced. Several decks opened onto the room, each one brightly lit and seemingly empty. If Richardson noticed any of this, he didn't let on. He focused on the person standing at the base of the tree.

The woman had long black hair pulled back into a frayed ponytail. She wore a gray jumpsuit, tattered and soiled at the elbows and knees. Her face looked gaunt, her eyes shadowed, but they shone with a fierce fire. Josiah had never met her, but this had to be Sanchez.

"It's about time you showed up." Her voice was a low growl, with enough fire to burn Josiah. "What did you do to my ship?"

"What are you talking about?" Richardson stomped toward her.

"Don't play dumb with me, Bruce. I know what you did here, setting all those traps. What did you do with my crew and ship?"

Richardson sputtered. Josiah stepped to one side, hoping to remain unnoticed. Overhead, the lights on one level flickered and went out.

"I didn't do anything!" Richardson's voice thundered through the atrium.

"Don't give me that! I don't know how you did it, that spooky voice that rattled my ship, the way my crew disappeared one by one, my ship vanishing too." Her gaze raked over the captain, her disgust palpable. "I always knew you were petty, but this—"

"Petty? You want to talk about petty?" Richardson stomped forward. "Who bribed that Federate patrol to impound my ship to get to the *Hemes Ascendant* first?"

Sanchez snorted. "All's fair, remember? Isn't that your motto?"

Josiah frowned up at the balconies overlooking the atrium. Another light had winked out.

"You learned well enough. You're always stealing my claims."

"Not my fault if you've slowed down, old man!"

Yet another light went out. Now darkness ringed the upper decks overhead. Josiah took a step back. "Uh, Captain?"

"This isn't about speed. You're not stealing the *Night Queen* from me. Get out!"

"Love to. Give me my ship back."

"I don't have your ship!"

Sanchez blinked, surprise painted across her face. "You don't?"

"No!"

The shadows overhead boiled, swirling like smoke. Josiah gagged on a bitter taste that suddenly flooded his mouth. He wanted to run, but his feet felt bolted to the deck. "Captain..."

"Then I got here first." Sanchez jammed her fist to her hips. "This wreck is mine."

Richardson's head snapped back as if struck. "Now wait just a moment. I paid a lot to a Federate tech crew to find this wreck, and I'm—"

"The crew of the *Farseer*? Technician Isaac Parker?" Sanchez laughed. She crossed her arms. "I bet I gave him three times as much."

"You—" The captain's face purpled and his hands clenched into fists.

The darkness had woven together, obscuring the dome. Josiah bumped into the wall behind him. The entire mass swirled and writhed, tendrils of shadow dropping lower, swiping at the air over the bickering salvagers' heads.

"You're not stealing this from me. The *Night Queen* is mine." Richardson yanked his weapon from its holster and leveled it at Sanchez. "I should have done this a long time ago."

Sanchez laughed. "You don't have the guts, old man. Never have, never—"

A crimson laser bolt flashed past her cheek. The shadows rumbled overhead. Sanchez spun around the tree, coming out with a weapon of her own. Richardson dove for cover as she unleashed a few shots.

"Captain..." Josiah edged for the door, keeping one eye on the darkness overhead.

Richardson ignored him and leaped from his hiding place. Sanchez emerged with a war cry, her weapon extended and ready to fire.

Then the darkness shattered, pouring down like water over the tree and the two salvagers. Richardson and Sanchez were knocked from their feet, swallowed up by shadows. Richardson shouted something at Josiah, but his words were overwhelmed by the roar of gale winds that practically ripped the tree from its perch.

Josiah froze, unable to move, as the waves of shadow swirled through the room, coalescing into a towering pillar. And then Josiah felt it, unseen eyes boring through him. The phantasm bent low, tendrils snaking from its body, grasping for Josiah.

A hunger rose up inside Josiah, a primal desire for more. More money, more respect, more of everything he deserved. A gasp burst from his mouth and he closed his eyes. He wanted the *Night Queen*. She was his, as she should be. He could strip her to the hull, sell everything he could find, and be rich beyond his wildest—

He shook his head and opened his eyes. The darkness hovered mere centimeters in front of his face, hot breath washing over him. Josiah fell back a step, searching for a way to get away.

There! The little boy was back, waving for Josiah from an open passageway. Josiah dove for the door, scooping up the child as he passed. The boy wrapped his arms around Josiah's neck and squeezed.

"It's going to be all right." Josiah hoped that wasn't a lie. He peeked over his shoulder. The shadow gobbled up the corridor. Rage, pure anger, screamed after them.

Josiah sprinted past doors that had somehow been restored to their original condition, as if Thompson had never blown them open. Josiah wished he could stop to take a closer look, to make sure his eyes weren't tricking him. But the darkness wasn't slowing. Its pressure nipped at his heels, cold clawed at his back and neck.

Josiah perked up when he saw the airlock. Just another twenty meters, and they'd be safe.

A wall of shadow burst from a nearby cabin, cutting off their escape route. Josiah dug in his heels and whirled, ready to run back, only to see the billowing column of darkness behind them.

Terror churned through Josiah's gut. This was it, then. He was surrounded, cut off completely. The darkness would devour him as it had Richardson and Sanchez. Probably Thompson and Sanchez's crew too. Worse, Josiah realized he deserved it. He was no better than the others, no matter how much he didn't want to believe it. He had been just as greedy. In spite of his misgivings, he too had hoped to find all kinds of riches on board. The only one innocent of all of this was the boy in his arms.

He scowled at the roiling darkness in front of him. "You can have me. But you can't have him. I won't let you."

A shadowy tentacle unwound, inching toward the boy.

"No! I said you can't have him!"

With a loud screech, the tendril disappeared into the darkness, which pulled open like a curtain, revealing an open corridor. Josiah stared down the hall. The path the probe had taken to the escape pods. Should he risk it?

He looked down at the boy. Yes, he should.

Josiah slunk down the hall, the darkness creeping along the wall on either side of him. Tiny wisps of shadow snaked out at them but didn't touch him or the boy. Josiah passed the spot where he thought the probe had been destroyed. Not a shard remained.

His strength bled through his legs with every step. By the time he made it to the escape pods, he was ready to collapse. He set the boy inside the nearest one and turned to face the darkness. It snapped and flared, its rage washing over Josiah. Once again, its siren call wafted through his mind. Josiah groaned as images of wealth and power flitted through him. All he had to do was stay. All he had to do was stay. All he had to do was...

His legs buckled beneath him, and he toppled backward into the escape pod. His head bounced off the cold metal floor, clearing his thoughts. He lunged for the large red button next to the door and mashed it with his fist.

The hatch sealed shut and with a muffled boom, the escape pod rocketed away from the *Night Queen*. The sudden acceleration tossed Josiah into one of the padded couches. He struggled against the g-forces to drag himself to a porthole and peek outside.

Light erupted across the *Night Queen*'s hull, so bright that Josiah had to shield his eyes with his hand. Then, an instant later, the light faded and when Josiah's vision cleared, the *Night Queen* had vanished along with the salvage vessel. Had the *Night Queen*'s engines propelled the wreck out of orbit? Or maybe the shadow had consumed the entire vessel. Either way, he breathed a sigh of relief and leaned back on the bench.

"So, do you have a name?" He turned to look at his companion, only to discover that the little boy had disappeared too.

Josiah stared at the empty bench. What the—? His mind churned with half-formed explanations as to where the boy had gone, but Josiah didn't want to consider any of them. He wrapped his arms around himself, leaned against the wall, and settled in for what could be a long wait.

Josiah lost count of how long he was in the escape pod. At first, he thought he'd have plenty to eat. The pod was designed to hold twelve and was stocked with enough food for that many passengers. But within hours, the food rotted away, crumbling to dust in Josiah's hands. What little remained smelled so horrible that Josiah didn't even want to touch it.

His stomach had turned into a painful knot by the time the Federate survey vessel came back to investigate Technician Parker's readings. The officers dutifully listened to his story, but Josiah could tell that they didn't believe him. Truth be told, he didn't really believe the story himself.

They brought him back to the nearest port, dropping both him and the escape pod in an empty cargo berth. When he asked, they explained that the pod was his rightful salvage.

Josiah was standing next to the pod, wondering what he was going to do with it, when a dapper looking older man in a gray suit approached him.

"You wouldn't happen to the boy who claims he found the *Night Queen*?" the man asked.

Josiah frowned at him. "I just got here. How did you hear about me?"

"Gossip travels faster than the speed of light in ports like this, especially when the news pertains to the *Night Queen*. My name is Erik Chandler." He produced a business card. "I represent a man who is interested in all things related to the doomed starliner. When he heard you were in possession of a life pod, he demanded I make an offer immediately. Providing, of course, that the pod is genuine."

"See for yourself." Josiah waved at the pod.

Chandler crawled over every square centimeter of the pod. At first, he wore his skepticism openly, but as his examination continued, his demeanor changed. By the end, sweat beaded his forehead and his hands trembled as he took notes on a personal data recorder.

"It would...it would appear that this is indeed what you claim." Chandler mopped his brow with a white handkerchief. "I am authorized to negotiate on behalf of my client. I'm sure that we can come to an equitable—"

Josiah held up a hand, cutting him off. "Name a price."

Chandler scribbled a number on a scrap of paper and handed it to him.

"Done." Josiah tucked it into his pocket.

Chandler hesitated. "Don't you even want to see what the offer is?"

Josiah shrugged. "I'm sure it's more than I'd ask for. Nice doing business with you."

Chandler smiled, glancing at the escape pod. "So what's next for you? Going out on another salvage run?"

"No way. I'm done with salvage runs. And if I were your client, I wouldn't go looking for the *Night Queen*. That kind of greed only consume you. Believe me, I know." Josiah turned and walked out of the bay. "Me, I'm going to buy the one thing I want most: a ticket home."

NOTES ON "THE NIGHT QUEEN"

THIS ONE IS ALL my friend Jill's fault.

Jill Williamson is an amazing author. I first encountered her when I read and reviewed her debut novel, *By Darkness Hid*, on my blog, *The Least Read Blong on the Web*. When I was getting ready to pitch my young adult superhero novel, *Failstate*, I wrote to Jill and asked her to read it for a possible endorsement. She not only endorsed it, but she also offered to introduce me to her agent when we attended a writing conference. And when Jill did introduce me to her agent, she also pitched the book for me, leading to me signing with said agent. Jill also helped me start teaching at the One Year Adventure Novel conference.

Well, Jill had been invited to write a short story for an anthology called *Spirited*. She knew that the editors were looking for another author so they could bring the total number of stories to thirteen, so she passed along my name, then asked if I could write a spooky story for the book.

Sure I could. Although I had never tried to write a scary story before... And I was trying to establish myself as a science fiction author... So what could I do?

I've been fascinated by the sinking of the *RMS Titanic* since I was in middle school. So I got this crazy idea of a spacefaring version of the liner that disappeared, a group of salvagers who stumbled across it, and why it might be a bad idea to mess with a place where everyone died. Thankfully, the editors liked the story, so it made it in.

So thanks, Jill!

FOCAL POINT

I'M EIGHTEEN AND I already hate my grandchildren. Maybe that's a bit harsh, but I just wish they would leave me alone. They always find a way to ruin the best moments of my life.

Like right now. I'm sitting in my room, cell in hand, trying to hang on to my courage long enough to actually call Melissa and ask her out. I've dreamt of this moment for weeks now, agonized over what I'd say. Her friends have been hinting that she wants me to call her. That's a minor miracle, so far as I'm concerned. I should be eager to make this call.

Except I know what's going to happen.

Oh well. Might as well get it over with.

As I tap in the first digit, an intense chill builds around me, like a polar vortex is parked in my bedroom. The hairs on the back of my arms dance. And the distinct smell of burning plastic claws at my nose.

With a soft *bloop*, a man wearing a sleek silver jumpsuit appears in my room. I don't know him, but I recognize the temporal displacement belt strapped to his waist. I've seen it on more than one occasion.

He turns a slow circle, his eyes wide. Then his gaze lands on me. "Curtis Higgs?"

I sigh and nod.

"I am Caesar Xavier Higgs the Sixteenth, and I have traveled back from the twenty-seventh century to..."

I tune him out. I've heard this spiel often enough. Instead, I study Caesar. He looks to be about thirty, a bit on the thin side, but I can recognize myself in him. He has my eyes.

They all have my eyes.

Caesar turns his head while making a dramatic point about his temporal voyage and I notice a metallic spider embedded in the side of his face. Huh. That's a new one. Wonder where he picked that up.

"—and that is why I have come." Caesar kneels down in front of me. "You must not ask out Melissa Stiles. Everything depends on it."

"What's that thing on your face?" I ask.

Caesar frowns at me. "Haven't you been listening to anything I said?"

"Sure, sure. 'You made the wrong choice, things have fallen apart, etcetera, etcetera.' What's that thing on your face?"

"It's my minder, placed there by my Cyberunion Overseer."

"And if I don't go out with Melissa, that will overthrow these tyrants?"

Caesar's frown deepened. "Why would you think that?"

Why would I? I keep hoping one of these "roads not traveled" would help save the universe or humanity or something. Hasn't happened yet, and apparently that's not why Caesar's here either.

"So why can't I go out with her?"

"It will skew your life and those of your descendants into a quagmire of pain and destitution. Believe me, Grandfather, this one small decision will have a profound effect on—"

"Fine, I get it." I toss the cell phone onto the bed next to me. "I won't call. Don't even know why I wanted to."

Except for the fact that it was Sylvie Higgs from the twenty-second century who suggested I check out Melissa in the first place. And Howard Higgs from the twenty-third told me to break up with Zoe Calderon after we had been going out for four months. That's just what they've done to my love life. Thanks to my grandkids, I've dropped and added so many classes my transcripts are going to be a mess. I've applied to, been accepted by, and then ultimately turned down at least a dozen colleges so far, all in the name of making things better for my descendants.

Caesar regards me through narrowed eyes. "That's it? No argument?"

I shrug. What's the point? I once spent twelve hours arguing with Zenomort X-7-Higgs from the thirty-second century about whether or not I should go to summer camp. He wouldn't leave until I tore up my application. I learned a long time ago that it's just better to do what my descendants want. Otherwise they won't leave.

"Very well." Caesar rises and places his hand on his belt. "Thank you, Grandfather. Your future family is grateful for your help."

He presses a button on the temporal displacement belt and with a soft *bloop*, he blinks out of existence, back to whatever utopia he thinks he created here.

I sigh. Why am I so lucky as to have these people visit me? None of my friends have their descendants popping in to offer advice on their life choices. So what gives? Maybe I'm the one who invented the time machine they're using. No, that can't be right. After the first half dozen visits, I made myself promise that I would never invent a time machine and I mean it. But that hasn't stopped them from coming.

I pull myself off the bed and head for the door. So much for Melissa. Might as well head downstairs and make some microwave popcorn, and then I can—

Bloop. "Curtis Higgs?"

I blow a long breath out of my nose. It's going to be long night.

Notes on "Focal Point"

Several years ago, some friends of mine started a flash fiction magazine called *Splickety*. Every issue features extremely short stories (the shorter the better) that are centered around a common theme. I kept my eye on what they were looking for, and one day, I noticed they were looking for stories about time travel for their blog.

So I started thinking about what kind of story I would want to tell. And I thought about the old grandfather paradox. You know, how you shouldn't go back in time and kill your grandfather since it'll erase you from history? Well, what if one person kept getting visited by his descendants, all of whom wanted to help make his life better? What if, every time he made a decision, he would be confronted by someone who told him he made a mistake and had to change his life to avoid a grim fate?

Sounded hilarious to me. And thankfully, my friends liked it too.

LIKE MANNA FROM THE HEAVENS

THE ENTIRE WORLD WAS watching and Wilson Zair was late.

He hurried past the reliefs, slipping through the middle of the holographic dome, and through the maze to the main entrance. His future was on the line here. But not just his. The world's too. The diplomats had lectured him about the gravity of today for months now.

He skidded to a halt outside the main entrance and quickly scanned the skies. No sign of the Alabrian shuttle. The sky above the temple was unusually empty, the traffic kept a respectful distance from the temple's airspace. Shuttles, military craft, and other vessels formed a loose halo on the edge of the no-fly zone.

But he knew what was up there, mixed with the traffic. Press drones. Hundreds, if not thousands, of flying imagers, all aimed at the temple. His late arrival was probably seen by billions of people, all watching this momentous event. The Hegemony and the Alabrian Collective were about to begin delicate trade negotiations and now, the Alabrians were coming here, to see the Dialectic. The pundits thought that today was just part of the diplomatic dance.

They didn't realize what the stakes truly were.

Wilson adjusted his robes, smoothed out his hair, and made sure that he looked every centimeter a respectful acolyte. Had to make a good first impression. They had been very clear on that point.

There. One craft broke through the ring and headed for the temple. No, drifted was a better word for it. Wilson frowned at it. In many ways, it looked like any other ship, long and narrow, with wings that arced from the top like waves on a beach. But the laws of physics seemed a burden to the Alabrian's shuttle, as if it slid through the air and barely tolerated gravity's pull. There was a wrongness to its motion, like it should be flitting sideways instead of forward.

As the ship started its descent, Wilson pulled the translation shell from his pocket. He turned it over in his hands several times, frowning at it. Made of a semi-translucent gel, it resembled a small jellyfish, and it felt slightly warm to the touch. Gritting his teeth, he slipped the device over his right ear. It immediately came to life, slithering along his skin and anchoring itself behind his earlobe, one tendril slinking into his ear. Wilson winced. He understood the necessity. Alabrian language was too complex for a human to learn; the translation shell could decipher the aliens' body language and coloration cues to give a richer understanding of not only what the Alabrians said, but what they meant as well. But it still felt as though a semi-frozen worm was trying to make its home in his ear canal.

"Keep it steady," he whispered. "Remember, they chose you for this honor." Some had wanted someone with more seniority to conduct the tour. But Wilson was the temple's senior acolyte. If anyone should do it, it was him. Eventually, the naysayers relented.

The Alabrian ship settled on the plaza in front of him with an audible thud, like it had dropped the final meter. A few minutes later, a hatch opened on its side, the metal melting and reforming into a bumpy ramp. Wilson frowned. Were those supposed to be stairs?

Then the first Alabrian emerged from the ship. Or rather, its carrying sled trundled down the ramp. The sled was a low-slung platform, one that hovered barely half a meter above the ground. Four short pillars rose from the corners of the platform, buzzing energy fields dancing between them. Thick mist filled the resulting bowl, spilling over the top and vanishing almost immediately.

And then Wilson saw his first Alabrian. The alien being swam through the air, its long form writhing and twisting as it occasionally dipped into the mist. Delicate arms, at least a dozen of them, were folded along the creature's length. Its head resembled a cross between a cat and an iguana, but with nine eyes forming a half-circle over its mouth. Its body was covered with fine hair that rippled in the afternoon sunlight, changing from green to red to a deep purple, waves of color crashing and mixing along the Alabrian's length.

Wilson's breath caught in his throat. It was hypnotic, beautiful. Not as much as the Dialectic, but very close.

Three more Alabrians emerged from the shuttle. They arrayed themselves behind the first and then the group slipped across the tarmac towards Wilson.

He plastered on the friendliest smile he could muster and bowed deeply at the waist. "Welcome to the temple of the Dialectic, honored guests."

"We appreciate the welcome and hospitality shown to us." The translator gave the lead Alabrian's voice a rich tenor quality, but then the device whispered, *Amusement; subtle mockery.*

Wilson risked a peek at the leader. Colors still spilled across the Alabrian's body and its body had slowed in its writhing. Several of its arms were cocked at angles that might have been painful on a human being. How the translator shell deciphered the emotional intent in that pose, Wilson had no idea.

"May I inquire as to whom I am addressing?" Wilson tried to bow even lower.

"I call myself Deep Searcher. My companions are Superior Senses, Scarred Carapace, and Clear Skimmer." *Prideful superiority.* "You are Wilson?"

"I am."

"Your leaders insisted we come here and see this 'Dialectic.' Take us to it. Now."

Wilson didn't need the shell's added *Authoritative command* to parse that. "Of course. It would be my pleasure." He straightened up and swept his arm toward the temple. "This way, please."

He stepped aside and the Alabrians floated past him. As they moved, their colors and postures shifted. The shell dutifully explained what he was seeing: *keen disinterest, mild resentment, restrained disgust.*

But one Alabrian paused by him. The creature studied him, its arms slack and a ripple of green and orange cascading along its fur.

Unabashed curiosity.

"Thank you for your hospitality." The shell rendered this Alabrian's voice as a high tinkling feminine. "I am called Clear Skimmer. I appreciate your time."

"It is my pleasure, my lady." Wilson bowed and this time, he meant it.

Genuine   pleasure. "We'd   best   keep   up   with my...first-male-parental-unit. He is unfortunately in a mood."

Wilson blinked, surprised at the hitch in the shell's translation. A word it couldn't render properly? Possibly. Whatever the case, he motioned for Clear Skimmer to go on ahead of him.

He followed the Alabrians into the temple itself. The entryway was cool and filled with shadows, a symbolic reminder of the dark times before the Dialectic's discovery. The corridor twisted and turned, often unexpectedly. It wasn't a problem for Wilson; he had walked this route numerous times and knew where to turn and when to step over the stumbling blocks strewn across the floor. The effect was for the pilgrims, and Wilson fondly remembered the first time he entered this sacred space. He had walked headlong into a wall, nearly breaking his nose. Painful, but it reminded him that—

"Why isn't there more light in here? Do you intend for us to ram into the walls?" Deep Searcher asked.

Wilson shook his head to banish the memories. "I apologize, sir. Most visitors find the effect—"

"We are not most visitors. Scarred Carapace! Fix this!"

Brilliant lights stabbed through the darkness, shining from the posts of one of the sleds. The unadorned stone walls were bleached out, practically white in the intense light. Deep Searcher grumbled something under his breath, which the shell didn't translate, although it helpfully added a *strong annoyance* to the mix.

"Perhaps we should move on to the holographic chamber," Wilson said.

"My apologies, Wilson," Clear Skimmer whispered. *Genuine embarrassment.*

He took the lead this time, guiding the delegation through the rest of the maze and to the next room. A large dome stretched overhead, its interior surface a shiny black dotted with small glass beads. A low barrier enclosed the center of the room, enough to discourage people from stepping inside the circle where the holograms would be displayed. It didn't stop Superior Senses from drifting to the center of the space.

Wilson motioned for their attention and smiled. "At this time, we would like to show you a brief documentary detailing the Dialectic's discovery." Wilson winced at the alliteration. Normally he wasn't so scatterbrained while leading a tour. Nerves. Had to be nerves.

The overhead lights dimmed. Thankfully, Scarred Carapace didn't take this as an invitation to turn on his floodlights again. Instead, subtle waves of color and light darted through the air, weaving together to form the whorl of the galaxy in the center of the room. Superior Senses squawked and retreated to the other side of the barrier. Orchestral music swelled and the image dove through a field of stars. Balls of light shot through the room, one buzzing close to Wilson's head, until the image came to rest on the planet Earth. The image shifted to that of old news footage, showing soldiers charging into battle, a drought-swept field dotted with scraggly wheat stalks, muddy water oozing in a riverbed.

"Three hundred years ago, chaos gripped the planet. Wars killed millions and, because of a century of rampant climate change, disasters were common place. Humanity was on a tipping point, about to pitch into extinction. But then, one lone explorer discovered an object that would transform our society, our planet, our very essence of being. This is her story."

The collage of disasters faded away, transforming into the dark void of space. Chunks of ice and rock tumbled through the air and a small shuttle pod, basically a battered gray metal teardrop, drifted among them. A ring of words formed above the floor and rotated slowly, declaring that what they were watching was a dramatic reenactment.

"Her name was Jenifer Pethick, a freelance asteroid prospector assigned to work the outer reaches of our Oort Cloud."

In a burst of light, they dove into the pod's cockpit, revealing Jenifer Pethick at the controls. The actress playing Pethick was pretty, although her face was tastefully smudged with grease. Her brown hair was pulled into a loose ponytail, although a few strands were loose to frame her face. If Wilson remembered correctly, this girl eventually went on to win a small army of Academy Awards for various holodramas. So far as he was concerned, this documentary was her best work.

As the actress worked the pod's controls, the voice of the real Jenifer Pethick took over the narration. "I had been out for a long time, at least six weeks, and I had come up pretty much empty. Lots of water ice, which was helpful, sure, but I was looking for heavy metals, rare elements, something that would help me pay off my debts to the guilds. I was desperate to find something...anything."

Wilson tore his gaze from the holo and checked on the Alabrians. While they still occasionally dipped into the mist in their sleds, they didn't tumble and twist quite as much, and it appeared as though they were watching the documentary. The shell deciphered their postures: *curiosity, slight boredom, hungry and tired, annoyance.* Clear Skimmer met his gaze and her fur rippled gold and silver: *warmth and camaraderie.*

A panel on the pod's control blatted and the actress leaned in to squint at it. The real Pethick explained, "And then the sensors picked up something they couldn't identify. They couldn't even tell if it was organic or metallic or what. I decided to investigate."

The holo pulled out of the cockpit and showed the pod drop lower to one of the ice chunks. Manipulator claws emerged from the craft and carefully pried the ice from the object, but thanks to the camera angles, the audience couldn't get a clear look at the Dialectic as it was wrenched free. Wilson swallowed a smile. That particular artistic choice often frustrated pilgrims, but it was deliberate to achieve a specific effect: those who built the temple wanted people to see the Dialectic with their own eyes, not as some simulation in a docuholo.

That was why the next scene unfolded the way it did as well. Pethick's face filled the room, a faint but growing glow playing across her features from beneath as her eyes widened.

"What I found was so much better than what I had set out to find." Every time Wilson heard Pethick's words, a shiver wormed up his spine. "It was like finding manna from the heavens."

"What is this nonsense?" Deep Searcher's voice cut through the swelling orchestral music. The Alabrian's sled hovered into the middle of the hologram. Lightning played across the sled's spires and, in a flash, the hologram was disrupted and vanished.

"Sir?" Wilson stepped forward. "What is wrong?"

"What's wrong?" *Incredulous anger.* "What's wrong, it asks? I'll tell you what's wrong. We have just arrived on this...obscure-gas-trail to negotiate with you up-jumped simians, but instead of starting the talks or letting us recuperate from the journey, you sent us here, to get us lost in dark mazes and force us to watch cheap entertainment!"

Wilson didn't need the shell to read the frustration in the ambassador's posture. His body writhed and twisted so much he was sure the Alabrian would wind up in a knot he wouldn't be able to untie.

"Come!" Deep Searcher's sled headed for the exit.

"Sir? Where are you going?" Wilson started after him.

"I am done with this ... false-jetstream-of-methane." The shell hitched and sputtered over Deep Searcher's words. "I am leaving."

No! A large block of ice lodged in Wilson's chest. Deep Searcher couldn't leave, not yet! He darted forward, coming around the Alabrian's sled and blocking its path with his body. "Please don't leave. I'm begging you."

"Scarred Carapace! Remove him." Deep Searcher's voice sliced through Wilson.

The other Alabrian slammed his sled into Wilson's stomach. Wilson fell back against the wall. As he recovered, the Alabrians slipped out of the room. Wilson tried to follow, but he was far enough back that the Alabrian's lights didn't help him. In his agitated state, he stumbled over the obstacles and even ran headlong into a wall. Pain exploded through his face.

By the time he stumbled out of the temple, he was too late. The landing ramp on the Alabrian's shuttle had retracted and, a few seconds later, the craft bounced into the air. Wilson stood on the edge of the landing pad, staring up at the retreating shuttle.

A few seconds later, a swarm of camera drones descended from the loop of ships circling the temple. The weight of the world's scrutiny pressed down on him and Wilson quickly retreated. He didn't want the world to see him. But deep in his heart, he knew it was too late. The Alabrians were gone. He had failed.

Prelate Tahan didn't even bother knocking before storming into Wilson's room. Well, not a room, really. More like a glorified maintenance closet. It still smelled of antiseptic and polish. The odor had even soaked into his cot. They kept promising him that they would move him to better quarters, but only when he proved himself. After today, he suspected this closet would be his permanent residence.

The prelate wasn't wearing his official robes, but that didn't make him any less intimidating. Wilson had never seen Tahan without a scowl on his hawk-like face, and this time, it was embedded so deeply Wilson wondered if it had been chiseled into place. The larger man paced back and forth in front of Wilson, who was sitting on his cot, his hands folded in his lap.

Finally, Tahan stopped and glared down at him, his copper eyes flashing. "Well? What do you have to say for yourself?" Wilson tried to speak, but Tahan cut off his words with a chop of his hand. "Do you realize how foolish we look? The Hegemony only wanted one thing from you: show the Dialectic to the Alabrians. How hard could that be?" Once again, Wilson started to answer, but Tahan wouldn't let him. "And now everything is in jeopardy. I have senior administrators threatening to punish me for your failure. What did you do?"

Wilson waited to make sure that the prelate actually wanted him to answer. When Tahan gestured sharply, he cleared his throat. "I did what I was supposed to. I took them through the maze. I tried to show them the documentary. But Deep Searcher didn't want to watch. I did everything I could to stop them."

Tahan seemed to deflate. "This is a disaster. Have you seen the news reports? Rumor has it that the Alabrians are preparing to pull out of the talks and leave Earth entirely."

Wilson's stomach clenched. This was worse than he had imagined. The Hegemony diplomats had drummed into him how important the talks were. If they had truly been derailed because of his failure, Wilson might as well get used to staying in this closet. Worse, he would probably be expelled forever. There had to be something they could do to fix this, to get what they needed...

Wait. The answer was right there in front of him the whole time, so obvious it was hiding in plain sight. Wilson leaned forward. "Prelate Tahan, excuse my impudence, but why don't we just ask them?"

Tahan's eyes bulged and he made a choking noise. "Wh-what?"

"I mean, why play these games? Why not just ask? What's the harm?"

"'What's the harm?' Do you understand how precarious our situation is right now? The Alabrian Collective has one of the largest fleets in this part of the galaxy and have trade connections with hundreds of species. They are ruthless in how they use both. If we were to show any sign of weakness, there's a good chance that they would take advantage of us. That's why the Hegemony decided to approach this the way they did."

While Deep Searcher was belligerent, Wilson had a hard time believing that Clear Skimmer would be that vicious. But if the Hegemony had made that determination, who was he to argue? He wasn't an expert on interstellar politics and never claimed to be.

"It doesn't matter anymore, I suppose. The opportunity is lost." Tahan sighed and shook his head. "Tomorrow the temple will re-open to the public. It has been determined that you will be assigned to the Hall of Reliefs to help with traffic control."

Wilson's head snapped back as if the prelate had struck him. That was a demotion, becoming little more than a glorified usher. He had been on track to become sexton. But this...this would end his upward climb.

Tahan's eyes sharpened. "You have some objection to this, acolyte?"

The words froze in Wilson's throat. The threat in the prelate's voice was clear enough. Tahan probably thought he was getting off lightly. Wilson dropped his gaze and shook his head.

"Very well. Report to the Hall tomorrow at 0730." The prelate started to leave but hesitated in the doorway. "For what it's worth, Wilson, you clearly weren't the right person for this job. We should have taken that into account. But then, maybe no one could have done any better. But we all must make sacrifices from time to time, yes?"

With that, Tahan slipped out of the room, leaving Wilson alone with his failure.

No one had noticed Wilson all day. He might as well have been just another decoration in the Hall of Reliefs. Maybe it was better that way. He couldn't decide which would be worse: to be ignored or to have people recognize him as the one who failed so spectacularly.

To help pass the time, Wilson let his gaze roam over the reliefs. Each had been carved into the walls, long ribbons of men and women emerging from the rock to commemorate the way they had contributed to the Hegemony. Each person had been inspired by the Dialectic to do great things. The pilgrims passed by the image of Jenifer Pethick, ensconced in her survey ship, only to encounter a three-meter tall sculpture of General Rajesh Narain, the visionary who first conceived of the Hegemony. Next to him were depictions of battles from the Time of Unity, which gave birth to a unified Earth. There was Dr. Tesia Lasek, who invented the quantum impulsion drive which had allowed human beings to spread throughout the solar system and beyond. Next to her was the enraptured face of Fale Tamura, the great artist who spent most of his life trying to capture the beauty of the Dialectic but always failed, and yet his failures were some of the most spectacular works of art in recorded history. And on it went: Raina Hernández, Cong Du, Nyree Heke, Shahrazad Sawaya, all of them giants who had been immortalized in the walls.

Wilson sighed. If yesterday had gone better, maybe it would have been his face etched into the stone for posterity. Wilson Zair, the man who built the foundation for an alliance with the Alabrians. But not anymore. Now he was relegated to a job a holographic signpost could have done. At least he still had his translation shell. Most of the pilgrims spoke Core, but a few of the old timers clung to their original cultures and yammered in various languages and dialects. The shell easily deciphered their words. None of the old timers had spoken directly to him, not yet, but at least he knew he would have the ability to speak to them if the need arose.

How much longer could this day last? The line of pilgrims moved a steady rate, each person shuffling toward the annex. Wilson idly wondered at the stories that each person carried with them. How many were coming for another glimpse of the Dialectic? How many were here for the first time? How many people hoped that this encounter would be enough to turn their lives around, the way the Dialectic had for so many? Wilson sighed. He had believed that as well, and now—

A ripple of murmurs passed through the crowd. Several of the pilgrims stopped their forward progress and turned around, gaping at something further back in the line. Wilson frowned. He stepped forward, clearing his throat, so he could urge them to keep moving.

"Hello, Wilson Zair."

The melodic voice took him by surprise and Wilson whirled to his left. An Alabrian sled hovered next to him, and even though the aliens looked so similar to each other, he knew immediately that it was Clear Skimmer. A thrill shot through him. What was she doing here?"

Sincere amends and embarrassment. "I have come to apologize for the behavior of my...first-male-parental-unit. He was out of line yesterday and should have behaved as befits his rank and authority. He treated you poorly."

Wilson's mouth popped open. What should he say in response? Simple honestly seemed safest. He bowed slightly at the waist. "Thank you for the apology, but I can understand why he—"

"No excuses for him. He is old and too quick to temper." *Amusement.* "Do humans behave the same?"

"Some do, my lady."

The sled rotated slowly and Clear Skimmer stopped her constant writhing dance through the mist. Her gaze seemed to flicker across the reliefs. Wilson struggled with the urge to explain what she was seeing. Maybe it was better to just let her take it all in herself.

"I had to come back and see the Dialectic myself."

"I'm sorry for the crowds, my lady." Wilson motioned for the pilgrims to keep walking. Far too many had stopped to gawk.

"Do not apologize. Seeing more of your people in the temple has helped me understand it better. The maze represents your struggle toward enlightenment, yes?"

Wilson smiled and nodded.

Warm satisfaction. "I thought as much. The unevenness of the floor was lost on me due to the antigrav sling, but I figured it out when I watched the pilgrims. And the documentary showed me what a difference the Dialectic has made for your people. And this place?"

Wilson considered his words carefully. True, this wasn't an official visit and seemed much more relaxed, but when word got out about this, he was sure that his every utterance would be dissected. "These are the men and women whose accomplishments were inspired by the

Dialectic. We commemorate the way they contributed to society in these displays."

"I see." *Open curiosity.* "When I came back to the temple, I had hoped to only see the Dialectic. I am glad that I had another opportunity to encounter you." *Warm affection.*

Wilson looked down into the eyes of Clear Skimmer and warmth spread through his chest. It was so strange, to find such an easy connection with someone he just met the day before, let alone a being from another planet. But why shouldn't that happen, and especially here? The Dialectic had created greater wonders than this little miracle. He felt so open, so comfortable, more than he ever had in the presence of another person.

In that moment, Wilson knew. The Hegemony didn't have to be so wary of the Alabrians. They could be open with them. Honest. Why hide behind the games and machinations?

"Wilson, is everything all right?" *Genuine concern.*

"Everything...everything is fine." He took a deep breath to calm his stomach, which felt like it was about to bore its way out of his body. "Clear Skimmer...is there any way you can convince your father to come back?"

"Why?" *Gentle teasing.* "Are you that anxious to be verbally abused again?"

"No, it's not that. I—that is, *we*—need him to see the Dialectic."

"Why?" *Wary curiosity.* "While he may have been rude, what he said was true. My people do not need to see the Dialectic to negotiate with yours. While I am curious to see it myself, we do not see the benefit in—"

"It's not to benefit you. It's..." He swallowed hard. Time to dive off the precipice. "We need your help."

"Whatever for?"

"To tell us what the Dialectic actually is."

Clear Skimmer went still in her sled. The shell helpfully explained her posture as one of *stunned surprise*, but Wilson had already figured that out. He glanced around to make sure none of the pilgrims heard his admission. Technically, he had just violated his orders from the official visit, but he felt so much lighter, so much freer for saying that out loud.

"You...you don't know what the Dialectic is?" *Cautious curiosity.* "The object that inspired your culture and technology?"

Wilson leaned forward so he could whisper. "We don't have any idea. Our finest minds have spent the past three hundred years examining it, and we simply can't figure out what it is or what it's supposed to do. We know it's an alien artifact, but that's it."

"So the reason you invited my father here—"

"—was to see if he recognized it. We know that the Alabrians have seen so much more than we have." He twined his fingers together. "I was supposed to show Deep Searcher the Dialectic and try to coax him into telling me what it was."

"Why didn't you just ask us?"

Wilson laughed, a mirthless bark. "Politics. A desire to not appear weak."

"Ah." *Sharp annoyance.* "I understand that...prevailing-current-of-helium all too well."

She fell silent, turning to look at the reliefs once again. Wilson tensed up next to her. What was she thinking? How would she answer? He felt like his body was falling through ice water, his head spinning and spinning and...

"All right." *Unease.* "I don't know if I can convince him. Deep Searcher can...fly-against-known-currents. But I will try."

"Thank you. And, if at all possible...can you please not tell Deep Searcher that we don't know what the Dialectic is?"

Warm acceptance. "Of course. Tomorrow, then?"

Wilson nodded. Clear Skimmer studied his face, and her body twisted into a corkscrew shape. Gentle whorls of blues and greens drifted across her fur. The shell stuttered, spitting out random sounds. He frowned. What did that mean? But then Clear Skimmer's body relaxed, her arms twitching into sharp angles. *Confused disappointment.* Her sled turned and slipped back out of the Hall of Reliefs.

Tomorrow. It felt like it would be an eternity, but maybe, just maybe, they would finally get the answers they needed.

Prelate Tahan was not happy when Wilson told him what he did. But what was done was done. The rest of the night was spent in a flurry of preparations. The Hegemony diplomats had to be contacted. Thankfully, Tahan left out the fact that Wilson directly asked Clear Skimmer what the Dialectic was. The prelate probably thought that the Hegemony would blame him, not Wilson. And while the diplomats weren't happy with the change in itinerary, they were more than willing to adjust their schedules for something this important.

Not everything went as smoothly as Wilson had hoped. They wouldn't be able to close the temple to the public the way they had the first time. There simply wasn't enough time. But in Wilson's mind, it was better that the Alabrians would be there with more people. Maybe Deep Searcher's behavior would be reined in with the presence of an

audience, and maybe he'd even see how important the Dialectic was if
he interacted with the other pilgrims.

Wilson didn't sleep the entire night, but in spite of that, he felt more
alive than he ever had, like he had been plugged in directly to the temple's power supply. He practically vibrated as he waited by the shuttle
landing pad. Once again, the Alabrian's shuttle descended from the
sky, but this time, Wilson wasn't alone. A line of pilgrims who waited
to enter the temple gawked at the ship. The shuttle touched down
and disgorged its passengers onto the tarmac. This time, Wilson strode
forward and bowed to Deep Searcher.

"You honor us with your presence again, sir."

The Alabrian leader made a noise the shell interpreted as a snort.
"My ... argon-river-chasing ... purported-female-progeny is to thank
for my return. Talk to her." *Annoyance.*

Wilson glanced at Clear Skimmer. Her twisting form looked like a
pretzel, jagged black and gray lines darting across her body and down
her arms. The shell deciphered it as *nervous anticipation*. He nodded
in her direction, then stepped aside, sweeping his arms toward the
entrance. "If you would follow me, please?"

The pilgrims in the line grumbled a bit as the Alabrians approached, but Prelate Tahan had sent burly ushers to force an opening in the line. Wilson led them through the maze, taking the most
direct route possible. As they walked, Clear Skimmer explained the
symbolism to Deep Searcher. The Alabrian leader didn't comment,
but at least he wasn't grumbling this time. And they didn't watch
the documentary either, skirting around the edge of the room as
the other pilgrims watched as various world leaders lauded Jenifer
Pethick's contribution to humanity. Then it was through the Hall of
Reliefs. Deep Searcher actually seemed to hesitate in front of some

of the displays, especially that of General Narain. But whatever Deep Searcher was thinking, the translation shell didn't decipher.

"Perhaps it is time to see this Dialectic." Deep Searcher shifted in his sled to face Wilson. *Hesitant curiosity.*

Not a clear win, but good enough. Wilson led the way. Once again, the ushers had to clear a path.

The Hall emptied into the central annex, a bowl-shaped room. The pilgrims stood in an orderly line, their path descending in loops. Thick pillars surrounded the central dais, more to obscure the pilgrims' view of the Dialectic than to support the ceiling. Ethereal music, mostly wind chimes and tinkling bells, wafted through the room. It was supposed to help stoke the visitors' anticipation in coming face-to-face with the Dialectic, but many considered it an unnecessary distraction. What did the Alabrians think of it?

Deep Searcher's sled bumped into Wilson. *Grudging admiration.* "This is all very impressive, but will we have to wait in line with...the drift-stealing-floaters? The odor here...it is unpleasant. Even more so than two days ago."

Wilson struggled to keep from grinding his teeth. Many of these "drift stealing floaters" had waited their whole lives for the chance to see the Dialectic. It didn't feel right to delay them, even for a few moments, for the surly Alabrian. But this was for the good of the Hegemony. He nodded to the ushers, who formed a wedge and started coaxing the waiting pilgrims to get out of the way. A chorus of angry whispers broke out in their wake, but Wilson did his best to ignore them. Hopefully Deep Searcher wouldn't understand the foul things being said about him. The last thing they needed was for him to bail a second time.

The Alabrian party slowly descended the ramps. As they walked, Wilson decided it was probably best to keep quiet, to just allow the aliens to experience seeing the Dialectic on their own for the first time. The architecture of the annex was designed to heighten the anticipation. Strategically placed pillars and banners obscured direct views of the central dais until they made a sharp right turn to walk the final few meters. As they approached the turn, Wilson sucked in a deep breath and held it. He loved this part of the experience: simply walking along, making the final turn, and...

There it was. The Dialectic. It wasn't all that large, a meter and a half tall, half a meter wide, and maybe a meter in diameter. Wilson could never properly describe its shape, for the Dialectic's form slowly shifted. One day, it might resemble a large potato, bulbous and rounded. Other days, it would have sharp edges and straight lines. Today, it had grown what looked like ridged conduits weaving in and out through the rest of the Dialectic, which resembled a chunk of rock. The one thing that didn't change was its color. It was always the same shiny black, a rainbow coruscating across its surface. A warm tingle swept from Wilson's head to the soles of his feet. Every time he saw it, he felt as though a part of his very soul came to life.

His party came to a halt behind a bright yellow line on the floor. They would have to wait there to approach the Dialectic while the pilgrim ahead of them had his time with it. But they had a clear view of the wondrous object. The Alabrians made a strange noise, one the shell couldn't translate. They were likely feeling the same overwhelming sense of awe he was.

An elderly man tottered up to the Dialectic. When he was only a meter away from the pedestal, he dropped to his knees. Wilson could hear his weeping from where he stood. Then the pilgrim stood up and crossed the distance, leaning in to delicately kiss the Dialectic.

"What is he doing?"

Deep Searcher's pained cry snapped Wilson's head around to the Alabrians. All of them thrashed in the mist in their sleds. Riots of colors and hues slammed together over their fur. The shell deciphered their body language as quickly as it could: *revulsion, horror, disgust.* What was wrong? Why were they so upset?

"Get us out of here!" Deep Searcher commanded. "Now!"

Wilson started moving before the words fully registered. With the help of the ushers, they hustled the Alabrians around the Dialectic toward the exit on the opposite side. The Alabrians maneuvered their sleds so they would stay as far away from the Dialectic as possible. They rushed through the corridor and out of the temple into the bright sunlight.

"What is wrong with you?" Deep Searcher asked. *Shocked outrage.* "Why would you do that?"

Obviously Deep Searcher knew what the Dialectic was, but why was he so upset? The rest of the Alabrians, including Clear Skimmer, were similarly agitated. They hadn't settled down since emerging from the temple. But this was the best chance Wilson had. "Do what?"

"Enshrine that...that *thing* like that."

"The old one touched one of his orifices to it," Superior Senses added. *Nauseous.*

The other Alabrians scooted their sleds away from Superior Senses's.

"I had no idea...honored-male-progenitor." Clear Skimmer said. *Ashamed horror.* "I didn't know."

"It is not your fault, child. The shocking ignorance of these barbarians in no ways reflects on you."

"What is wrong?" Wilson took a step toward Clear Skimmer. "Why are you all so upset?"

"How can you not be? How can you so proudly display that abomination like that? Don't you know what that is?"

Wilson looked to Clear Skimmer for help. She wouldn't meet his gaze.

Deep Searcher gasped. "You didn't know what it was, did you?" *Shocked disbelief.* "It is coprolite. *Lintarian* coprolite."

Wilson stared blankly at Deep Searcher.

"Tell me, human, do your people enshrine everyone's excrement?"

Wilson's heart collapsed into his feet. "Y-you mean...the Dialectic is..."

Reluctant agreement. "It is, Wilson. I'm sorry," Clear Skimmer said.

Wilson collapsed onto the ground, staring at the Alabrian sleds. "I don't understand. Why would we find that in our solar system?"

Deep Searcher snorted. "I'm not surprised. The Lintarians were notorious for spreading their secretions throughout the galaxy. And they were prodigious at creating it, that is certain. If they hadn't gone extinct eons ago, the entire universe would have been stuffed to bursting with their refuse."

"It is said that the Lintarians were the cloacae of black holes," Scarred Carapace muttered. *Disgust.* "That's the only way they would have been able to produce so much."

"Their leavings have fouled entire solar systems. It is incredibly toxic and..." Deep Searcher's voice trailed off. *Thoughtfulness.* "How long have you humans had this 'Dialectic' of yours?"

"Three hundred years," Wilson whispered. Three centuries, and they had no idea...

"And the elderly human...he kissed it," Deep Searcher added. "I assume others have done the same in the past? With no ill effects?"

"None." Wilson thought of the many times he had come close to touching the Dialectic himself. He never had, not wanting to sully something so precious.

Deep Searcher's body stilled. He still twisted and rotated above his sled, but he moved in slow motion, his arms stroking the length of his body, which turned a uniform bright orange. *Deep thought.* After a few minutes, he moved faster, his coloration changing rapidly.

"We must go speak with your diplomats, human," Deep Searcher said. *Crafty determination.* "We need to begin negotiations. I believe I have an idea for a trading arrangement that your people will find more than fair."

Scarred Carapace and Superior Senses turned bright orange, and then made a noise the shell rendered as chuckling.

"Sir! No, you cannot!" Clear Skimmer said. *Abject horror.*

"Oh, yes." *Satisfaction.* "I believe we can work out something that will be mutually beneficial."

The skies over the temple were clear, as they usually were. But they wouldn't remain that way for long. After all, the Alabrians were coming.

Wilson winced at the pain in his knees and back. He knew he shouldn't be sitting on the tarmac, that he would ache for hours afterward. His doctor had said as much during his last physical. And his children and grandchildren, oh, how they pestered him to leave. *"No one goes to the temple anymore. Not for years and years. Why stay?"*

He couldn't answer them. They could never understand. The Dialectic had uplifted humanity when it was discovered. And then it changed their collective fate again when the Alabrians saw it fifty years ago. Where else could he be?

Something crunched through the ashes behind him, the unsteady tread of someone walking. Wilson frowned. Apparently the temple could still attract some pilgrims. But why would they come on the same day as the Alabrians?

"I can't believe it!" The voice was young, enthusiastic, and the owner matched. He couldn't have been more than twenty, maybe even younger. A holocam hovered over his left shoulder, the small orb spinning in the air to scan the surroundings. "It's true. You're...you're *real*!"

"Last time I checked," Wilson said.

"No, I know that, but...but you're him, aren't you? Wilson Zair? You were the one who spoke to the Alabrians, the one who first learned what the Dialectic is." He stretched out his arms, indicating the decaying cityscape that stretched out before them. "People say you're the one who caused all of this!"

People did say that, and worse. Wilson's gaze skipped over the crumbling buildings that surrounded the temple, all of which bore scars from decades of bombardment. Smoke continually rose to the sky, remnants of humanity's attempts to cope with the Alabrian's trade deal. Nothing worked.

"I'm so lucky to have found you! See, I'm doing this documentary for school about the Dialectic and so I figured I'd come here, film it while it happens, but now I've found you! How incredible is that?"

Wilson sighed, deep enough it rattled his ribs. To be that young and enthusiastic again, the way he had been when he first saw the Alabrians.

When he first saw her.

Thunder rolled across the landscape, but there were no clouds. Wilson looked up. The Alabrians had arrived.

There was no sign of them, not at first, but then dozens of freighters burst into existence in the sky. Then, in unison, they opened their holds and dumped their cargo. Wilson had seen them do this hundreds, maybe thousands, of times. Loads of Lintarian coprolite, falling to earth, great waves of it thundering down to the ground.

Deep Searcher's proposal had been quite simple: humans, who revered the Dialectic, would be given as much coprolite as the Alabrians could gather, and the deliveries wouldn't cost them a thing. Now people didn't have to travel to the temple anymore. On a regular schedule, their own personal copies of the Dialectic would arrive on their doorstep. And the Alabrians assured them that the other species in the galaxy were oh so grateful for the humans' contribution. It was a win/win.

The young man laughed. "Look at it all! There it is, old man! Your legacy."

Tears stung Wilson's eyes. What Jenifer Pethick had said all those centuries earlier was true. She described the Dialectic perfectly.

It truly was like watching manna fall from the heavens.

NOTES ON "LIKE MANNA FROM THE HEAVENS"

THIS ONE MIGHT TAKE a little bit of explanation.

Technically, this was another Kickstarter story. I found a guy putting together an anthology about alien artifacts. What would happen to human civilization if someone found an alien artifact somewhere? How might humanity improve itself? Or would we tear ourselves apart?

As I read about the project, a different question occurred to me: what would happen if we didn't know what it was? What if we never figured out what it was? And since I'm a big fan of twist endings, what if, when we found out what it actually was, it turned out that we had made a horrifying mistake? The idea for the Dialectic immediately sprung to mind and I laughed myself silly as I wrote the story. Sadly, it wasn't chosen for the anthology.

So why did I call this one "Like Manna from the Heavens?" Well, because years ago I learned something interesting about the story of God providing the people of Israel with manna in the wilderness. For those of you unfamiliar with the story, after Moses led the people of Israel out of Egypt, they wandered through the desert for forty years. As you might imagine, they were not thrilled with this development and they started to complain about it, particularly about the lack of food. So God performed a daily miracle: just about every morning, a flaky substance could be found on the ground in the Israelites' camp. They coudl gather up enough for the day and thus, they didn't starve. And they called this miracle food "manna."

But why did they call it manna? Because in Hebrew, the word *manna* means "What is it?" They had no idea what this stuff was, and the commemorated their ignorance by using that phrase to name it.

I thought it was an interesting connection with the Dialectic, especially how the story ends. So I decided to include a little Hebrew joke in the title, just for me.

Homecoming

Another dead planet drifted past on the navigation display, a husk of stone and ash orbiting a flickering star. I had seen so many at that point in the journey I didn't bother to log it. No one at the home office would care; they all knew that the Expanse was populated with barren worlds and dying stars. The *Atwood* had already skimmed past a dozen similar planets and, if the old charts I had pulled up from the early explorers were true, we could see at least a dozen more before this mission was over. While the lack of hospitable worlds didn't bother me much, the same couldn't be said for the rest of the *Atwood*'s crew.

"It ain't right, Cap'n." Jones didn't turn from the navigation controls. "This many barren planets, all clustered together in one region. Ain't right. Ain't *natural*."

I rolled my eyes. Thankfully we were the only ones on the bridge to listen to the navigator's latest rant. Maybe if I ignored him, he'd settle down. I called up the ship's status to distract me. I scrolled past three messages from our only passenger. He was likely trying to remind me that we were behind schedule. Life support, nominal. Engineering, within recommended tolerances. Security, all secure.

Apparently Jones took my silence as an invitation to continue. "Everywhere else in the galaxy, you find all sorts of planets. Big'uns and littl'uns, some rocky, some gassy. Some with water, some dry. But you don't see so many dead worlds, not like this. Why we gotta go here, Cap'n?" He swiveled in his chair and fixed me with a pointed look, as if daring me to disagree.

Far be it from me to disappoint him. "You're being paranoid, Jones."

Jones shook his head so rapidly it looked like he was having a seizure. "No, the Expanse is cursed and I know it. We should turn around and head back to port. Now!"

I pinched the bridge of my nose to stave off a mounting headache. "We can't do that, Jones, and you know it. We've got a contract and we can't break it just because the Expanse gives you the shakes."

Maybe that wasn't the most polite way to phrase it. Jones stiffened in his chair and launched into a string of old spacers' tales, how uncountable ships had disappeared or were destroyed or the crews all went mad when they dared to venture into the Expanse. I did my best to tune him out as I continued to scroll through the ship's status. All departments except for medical had checked in with nothing to report. I was about to show the list to Jones just to shut him up, but I hesitated and scrolled through the list again. Medical hadn't reported in at all. I frowned. That wasn't like Dr. Mendenhall. Even if the crew was completely healthy, she would at least log her presence in the medical bay. It was worth checking, if for no other reason than to give me an excuse to leave Jones to his rambling paranoia.

"I'll be back in a sec." I hauled myself out of my chair and left the bridge, not waiting for Jones to respond.

My eyes had trouble adjusting to the shadowy corridor outside of the bridge. Our passenger had insisted on dimming the lights considerably during the trip. Something about power levels and energy fields or something like that; I left the details to Chief Engineer Daniels to manage. We've dealt with stranger requests in the past, but somehow, the darkness muted the rest of the ship, swallowing the sounds and vibrations and colors.

I shook my head. Ridiculous. I had let Jones get into my skull.

The doors to the medical bay parted before me and I stepped through into a darkened room. The room was empty and Dr. Mendenhall wasn't in her office. I glanced at my chrono. She should have logged in fifteen minutes ago. She was never late.

The doctor's quarters weren't far from the medical bay. Even though I figured Dr. Mendenhall was sleeping in or maybe even sick herself, I still hustled through the corridors. The sooner I could be back on the well-lit bridge, even if it meant spending more time with Jones, the better. The walls seemed to loom large in the shadows, and a strange scent, like that of mold mixed with salt water, tickled my nose. I frowned. Had the lack of power compromised the atmospheric scrubbers? Something to look into later.

I turned a corner and nearly slammed into our sole passenger. Mr. Henry Danforth looked like someone had animated a skeleton and stretched a thin layer of mottled skin over its frame. He was almost completely bald, save for a few wisps of hair that defied the ship's gravity. He wore suits that may have been fashionable sixty years ago, but each one I had seen was rumpled and dotted with old stains. He peered at me with his wet eyes and his lips twitched into an expression that was neither sneer nor smirk but some combination of both.

"In such a rush, Captain?" he asked. "Whatever could be the matter?"

"Just ship's business, that's all." I stepped around Danforth and kept walking. Hopefully he would catch the hint.

He didn't. Instead, he fell into step with me. "How much longer until we reach our destination, may I ask? It is imperative that we get there as soon as possible. After the delay with our departure..."

"Mr. Danforth." I stopped and faced him. "I understand your frustration. But it wasn't our fault that the ground crew was late in refueling the *Atwood*. We're doing the best we can, especially since we're venturing so deep into an uninhabited region of space." I frowned, some of Jones's earlier rantings tickling the back of my mind. "But if you don't mind me asking, Mr. Danforth, why are we taking you so deep into the Expanse? So far as we know, there's nothing to find here."

Danforth's eyes glittered as a smile tugged at his lips. "Ah, but you can only find if you know what you seek."

"And you do?"

"Of course. I am guided by wisdom in an ancient tome, one that has offered guidance to many over the centuries."

Oh, great. I should have known that Danforth would turn out to be a religious nutter. Who else would spend so much to transport one crate to the middle of a vacant region of space?

"I do hope that you will do your best to make up for our delay, Captain. It would be most...unfortunate if you didn't."

I ground my teeth, fighting to remain civil. "We are making our best possible speed. Now, if you'll excuse me, I have some urgent matters to attend to."

Both statements were lies, but Danforth seemed to accept them. I kept going and thankfully, he didn't follow.

When I arrived at Dr. Mendenhall's quarters, I pressed the signal button and waited. There was no answer. I tried again, this time counting the seconds while I waited.

Upon reaching two hundred, I tapped in my command override code into the lock. I could have been overreacting to nothing, but I figured better safe than sorry.

The doors to the doctor's quarters hissed open. As I stepped through, the lights flickered on, revealing a pool of blood. Then I saw her. Doctor Mendenhall slumped against a bench, her eyes were open and vacant.

I dropped down next to her and examined her body. She was dressed in her uniform, the front of which was stained with blood. A closer look revealed the source. Her throat had been slit. Metal glinted in her right hand, a surgical scalpel gripped in a fist. Had she killed herself?

"Oh dear."

I turned around. Danforth stood in the doorway, his gaze on the doctor's body. And for a brief moment, a look of worry crossed his face.

"Mr. Danforth, please return to your cabin." I shouldered my way past him back into the corridor.

Much to my relief, he didn't argue. Instead, he watched as the door to the doctor's quarters slid shut, then retreated without a word. I blew a breath out through my nose, trying to calm my stuttering heart. Maybe, just maybe Jones was right.

I couldn't tear my gaze from the blood.

The body had been removed an hour earlier by security. We didn't have a morgue on the *Atwood*, but one of the empty cargo holds could be refrigerated. Cargomaster Lewis promised it would work and I trusted her opinion. But with the body dealt with, that left the larger question looming over me.

Why was the doctor dead? I had last spoken to her... I wracked my brain. The night before? Yes, we exchanged a greeting as we passed in the commissary. She had seemed fine at the time, but then, isn't that what people say after a tragedy like this? I tried to remember my last in-depth conversation with her if only to parse her words for some hint that she was considering this. But the last time we had spoken, it had been all business. Come to think of it, we had never had what I would call a close relationship. Dr. Mendenhall had been a cipher to me the whole time.

Someone cleared his throat behind me. I turned and found Security Chief Olson standing with his hands clasped behind his back.

"What do you have for me, Chief?" I asked.

He stepped closer. "I did like you asked, Captain. Checked the security logs and asked around. Last anyone saw the doc was last night in the commissary. Security logs show her going into her quarters at 1800, and then nothing, not until you came in here this morning. Near as I can tell, no one even went through the corridor outside her quarters overnight. Looks pretty cut and dried to me."

So a suicide, then. I frowned. That didn't feel right. The thought of the doctor killing herself clashed with my scant memories of her, creating a dissonance that soured my stomach.

"How's the crew taking this?" I asked.

Olson scuffed at the floor. "Pretty shook up, all things considered. Took the liberty of having them assemble in the commissary. I figured they might need a few words from their captain."

I patted Olson on the shoulder and slipped out of the room. It took me a few minutes to walk to the commissary. As I went, I considered what I should say. I couldn't offer much comfort. If the doctor was religious, I had no idea. Besides, I was hardly qualified to officiate. Better to wait until we made it back to port for that sort of thing.

But that was the question: should the *Atwood* make Danforth's delivery or should we just go back? Continuing without a doctor was risky, but it wasn't against regulations either. And I trusted the crew to be careful in their jobs. And we were closing in on our destination, the heart of the Expanse. A few extra days wouldn't hurt the body.

A familiar scent, salt and mold, tickled my nose. I paused and breathed deeper, but it had vanished as quickly as I detected it. I frowned, but then shook my head and kept walking. By the time I reached me destination, I knew what we had to do.

Sure enough, the crew had gathered in the commissary. There were only two dozen of them, and they had clustered in smaller knots and talking quietly. As I stepped through the door, they fell silent and turned to me, their faces somber but attentive. Well, almost all of them. Jones sat at one of the table, slumped over and he seemed to be asleep. I cleared my throat, hoping he'd at least pretend to pay attention. No good. I ground my teeth. Maybe I'd have to talk to him. He was a senior officer; he should be setting a better example.

"Ladies and gentlemen, I'll keep this brief. We all have duties to attend to." My throat closed up and I swallowed the lump. "As I'm sure you've all heard by now, Dr. Gretchen Mendenhall has died. We are investigating what happened. While she was the newest member of our crew, she will be missed." Would that be good enough? It would have to do. I nodded. "All right. Back to stations. We will—"

"You're not really thinking of going on, Cap'n?" Jones looked up at me, fear painted across his face. "Not with a dead body on board. Not through the Expanse."

A murmur swept through the crew. My hands clenched into fists. I should have known that Jones would object.

The doors to the commissary slid open and Danforth stepped through. He skirted along the edge of the room, close the walls, his gaze locked on me.

"We are going on," I said. "We've made it this far. If we turn around now, we're only going to cost the company a lot of money in fuel and wages. And I have every confidence in this crew that we'll be fine without a doctor on board."

Jones shook his head. "I don't like it. This ain't right! None of it is right. All these worlds, sucked dry like old corpses. Whisperings from the shadows! We're not gonna make it."

I rubbed at my temples, trying to forestall the headache that I knew would build with this argument. Now the crew were whispering to each other, but if it was because they agreed with Jones or were disturbed by his ravings, I had no idea. A few of them inched away from him as if worried he would attack them.

All the while, Danforth's gaze kept boring into me.

"Enough!" The word burst from my mouth in a bark. "We're going. Jones, if you have a problem with that, you're relieved of duty and confined to your quarters." If the doctor were still alive, I would have ordered her to sedate him for good measure. "The rest of you, back to your stations."

Jones sputtered but didn't answer. Then he got up and, with a glare at Danforth, left the commissary in a rush. The rest of the crew followed, some of them casting sympathetic looks in my direction, others studying the floor as they walked.

I stepped forward and snared the arm of Chief Engineer Daniels. "A word, Chief."

He glanced at his team as they filed out of the room, then turned to face me. He was a young man, fresh out of university a year earlier. He'd been with us for the last six months. Good kid, all things considered, but still inexperienced. Maybe that was why he looked so nervous. I know I would have been too if someone died on my first posting like this.

"I know you've got the engines running at peak efficiency, but see if you can't eke out a little more power, okay?" I tried to phrase the order like a question if only to set him at ease. "I want to finish this run as quickly as we can. It'd be better for the crew, for the doctor's family, for all of us."

His jaw worked as if he were chewing on the request, but he still nodded. "I'll see what I can do, sir."

He started to leave but I caught his arm again. "One other thing. I want someone to check the atmospheric filters in life support."

He frowned. "Why?"

Couldn't he smell it, the tang of salt in the air? Did he think that was normal? Maybe he grew up in a coastal city and thought the air was supposed to smell like this. It didn't matter in the end. "Just double check to make sure everything is working, got it?"

"Yes, sir." He escaped through the door.

I took a few moments to breathe and compose myself, but even as I left the room, the memories of the doctor's blood and the scent in the air chased me through the corridors.

I bolted upright in my bunk, chest heaving. The strange visions of my dreams slowly uncoiled but the wailing remained. No, wait. Not wailing. Just the door chime. I frowned and rolled over to look at my clock. Who would bother me at 0300? I slid out of bed and grabbed a pair of pants, slipping them on as I stumbled over to the door.

It hissed open, revealing a young man in uniform fringed with the red stripes that identified him as part of security. According to his badge, he was Security Assistant Wesley Gilles. I frowned. Why would Olson have sent this rookie to wake me up?

"What is it, Gilles?" I injected a little bite into my words.

His entire body trembled and his eyes were wide. "Sir, you have to come. Now."

"Why?"

"There's been..." He swallowed and I suspected he was fighting to hold back tears. "It's Security Chief Olson...and Cargomaster Lewis. They..."

A weight settled into my stomach. "What? Spit it out!"

"They're both dead. Suicides."

I stared at him, unsure I heard him correctly. But then I snared a shirt from the chair near the door and followed him into the corridor. He led the way to Olson's quarters. As we walked, he tried to tell me what happened, but his words were a near incomprehensible babble. I think I understood the gist: sometime during the night, Cargomaster Lewis walked into the secondary cargo bay and blew the hatch. She had been sucked into the vacuum immediately. When Gilles tried to report the incident to Chief Olson, he discovered that Olson had used his sidearm to vaporize himself from the neck up.

No wonder the kid was scared. I would be too. I barely was able to hold down the rising tide of panic that threatened to sweep me away. But I had to remain in control. I was the captain. It was my duty.

A small knot of crew members had gathered around Olson's quarters. They parted as we approached. Gilles hung back as I walked through the door. He probably had seen enough already.

Sure enough, Olson's body lay in the middle of his room. His shoulders were covered with a scorch mark, his head and neck gone. I tried to remain impassive, to look for any indication of what had happened, but the weight in my stomach surged upward and I quickly stumbled out of the quarters and pitched into the far wall.

"What are we going to do, Captain?" Gilles asked.

I tried to formulate an answer, something I could tell him, but before my thoughts could order themselves, the deck underneath us bucked wildly. Emergency alarms blared through the halls.

I turned to the gathered crew. "To your stations!"

They bolted, hurrying out of my way. I raced through the corridors, heading for the bridge. With every breath, I choked on the musty smell that chased my steps. What had happened now?

I emerged on the bridge and jumped into my chair, calling up the *Atwood's* status. The board was awash in red light. Some sort of failure in the main generator. The engines were still working, propelling the ship through the Expanse. But what had happened?

My fingers flew over the controls as I called up the security feed from the generator room. A gray cloud swirled through the compartment, obscuring the view. Had a coolant line ruptured? I thumbed the intercom, calling up Chief Engineer Daniels. He didn't answer. Instead, gasps and feeble cries whispered from the speakers, their words overwhelmed with the sound of rushing air.

I closed the connection and rewound the footage on the security feed, back fifteen minutes. The cloud vanished in a blur and I played back the footage. The night crew, three men and a woman, worked at their stations. Everything looked normal, but then someone burst into the room, wielding a lit plasma cutter. The newcomer leapt onto one of the crew, slicing at them with the tool. It took me a moment to recognize the attacker as Daniels himself. The Chief attacked his crew, then turned the cutter's beam on a coolant line. My fingers dug into the arms of my chair as I watched the conduit burst, spewing the toxic cloud into the room. Daniels dropped the torch and collapsed to his knees, retching. And then he vanished as the coolant overwhelmed him.

"Cap'n."

I froze at the quiet word, then slowly turned in my chair. Jones stood at the entrance to the bridge. He cradled a laser rifle close to his chest and a wild fire burned brightly in his eyes.

"I told you, didn't I? We shouldn't have come to the Expanse. The worlds are dead and now, so are we. And I know why."

I didn't move, didn't dare even breathe. He wasn't aiming at me yet, but he could, probably faster than I could close the distance between us. The bridge's open design offered me few places to hide.

"It's because of whatever that Danforth brought on board. Don't you see, Cap'n? It's been floodin' the ship with doom and now it's going to destroy us all. Well, not if I don't destroy it first!"

He spun and lurched off the bridge. I gaped after him, surprised to still be alive. But then I bolted after him, chasing him through the corridors. He was headed for the main cargo bay, sure enough.

But then Danforth slammed into Jones, knocking him off course. The wiry man no longer wore his rumpled suit, but long black robes with a crimson fringe along the sleeves and hem. He held a dagger, its blade a corkscrew of metal with dark jewels on the hilt.

"I tried to warn you, Captain," he said. "I tried to tell you to hurry, that we couldn't be late, but you didn't listen, did you? And now it wakes. Yes, before it arrived home. And see what beauty it has wrought."

Jones roared a challenge and charged. Danforth whirled faster than I thought possible and plunged his blade into Jones's stomach and then pulled it free with a vicious shout. Jones staggered and gasped, his hand fumbling at his wound. The rifle clattered across the deck and came to rest at my feet.

I quickly scooped it up and turned it on Danforth. The man dropped to his knees and laughed. He actually laughed!

"It is too late, you see? I tried to protect us as best I could, but the dreams of a god cannot be contained when it stirs."

"You're insane!"

He shook his head. "No more so than any who dare to walk in the shadows of giants."

He lunged for me and I pulled the trigger, the crimson beam slicing through Danforth's chest. He toppled and fell on top of his dagger. A pool of blood slowly spread out beneath him, staining the deck. He didn't get up again.

My fingers tightened on the rifle. As much as it pained me to admit it, Jones was right. Whatever it was that Danforth brought onto my ship had to be destroyed. Maybe the rifle wouldn't be enough, but maybe I could vent the hold, dump it into the Expanse. I had to at least try.

I sprinted the rest of the way, the corridors strangely empty. I wondered what had happened to the rest of the crew, if they were huddled in their quarters, scared or perhaps slowly descending into madness. Had they killed themselves as well? No. Focus! Deal with the threat first, then evaluate the damage.

I skidded to a halt outside the cargo hold. After taking one last shaky breath, I opened the door.

A wave of salty air mixed with the choking odor of mold washed over me and I staggered backwards. What felt like a vice tightened around my head and a cry ripped free of my throat. I clawed at my temples, trying to dislodge the pressure. But it only grew, driving me to my knees. I gagged as the scent overwhelmed me.

As I knelt there, I heard it, the wet sound of leather scraping against metal, drawing closer and closer to me. I risked a look and how I wish I hadn't! For a shape, monstrous and overwhelming, towered over me, its mottled skin glistening in the dim light. It wasn't human, that much I understood, but as I tried to decipher its form, the pressure in my brain increased, becoming more intense as a high-pitched keening mixed with my own screams and I wanted nothing more than to shrivel up.

But no. Visions of blood mingled with the odors of salt dragged me under and the riptide sent me tumbling through visions of buildings trapped in ice, their angles impossible and disturbing, the inhabitants of those ancient walks even more so. And I kept falling and falling until darkness reached up and smothered me in its depths.

They tell me that the *Atwood* drifted out of the Expanse three weeks later. A scavenger vessel found her, life support barely functioning, all the holds open to space, and I was the only survivor. The ship's computers had been scrubbed, and all of the navigational data was erased. The crew and Danforth were gone. Me they found in my bunk, a gibbering wreck, spouting words with no meaning and staring at the ceiling. The only clue as to what happened were puddles of briny water in the main cargo hold, indicating the *Atwood* may have landed in an ocean at some point. I didn't know. I couldn't remember.

I spent close to a year in a psychiatric institution, where the doctors worked to knit together my damaged psyche. They eventually succeeded, and they believed me when I said I couldn't remember anything that happened on the voyage. I suppose they were relieved they wouldn't learn the truth.

Wise men. I wish I could forget. But even now, as I sit in my home, I can still smell it, the salt and the mold. As if the odor clings to me, like rot on a corpse. The memories will not leave me either. I must live with the deaths of my crew, for that was the price, it seems, to bring Danforth's creature home.

NOTES ON "HOMECOMING"

LIKE I SAID EARLIER, I don't write spooky stories all that often. I don't read them either. I'm not a big horror junkie, although I do have a soft spot for found footage movies. I don't know why, I just do.

That doesn't mean that I'm unaware of scary stories. And that's especially true of the work of H. P. Lovecraft. I've seen dozens if not hundreds of references to his creations. Eventually, I decided I wanted to educate myself more on Lovecraft's work, so I went to a used bookstore and picked up an anthology of his stories and read the thing cover to cover. Some of them were great. Some weren't. Most of them showed Lovecraft's despicable prejudices. But after reading the anthology, I decided I wanted to try my hand at a Lovecraftian story. But I decided to give it a sci fi twist.

Did I succeed? I have no way of knowing for sure. I think so. Apparently I did well enough to sell it to an online magazine, so I guess there's that.

IN THE SHADOW

MY SON WOULD HAVE loved this new old world. I'm just thankful he didn't live to see it.

I scan the surrounding buildings. This was a nice suburb, once, but now the houses are decaying. Smoke rises in the east like a finger trying to gouge out the sun.

"Boss?"

Glancing over my shoulder, I see Halloway standing in the open doorway. I nod toward the east. "I didn't order a burn. What gives?"

Halloway grimaces. "Patrol found walkers nesting in the old school. Structure was too far gone to salvage."

I groan. Third building we've lost on the perimeter. Might have to move soon. "Quiet night otherwise?"

He shakes his head. "New batch of refugees came knocking. Got 'em in Q now. No obvious bites or scratches, but..." He fidgets with something.

"What?"

"One of 'em had this."

He hands me a laminated ID card: Anastasia Corp.

"So we got an Anie," I say. "That's nothing new."

Halloway taps the badge. "Check the name and title, boss."

I do and my heart stutters. Dr. Miguel Florez, Chief Research Officer. An Anie scientist? And one of the top guys, too?

He nods grimly. "Thought you might want to have words with him."

That's putting it mildly. I shoulder past Halloway into the compound and my gaze sweeps over the walls. More cracks. More water trickling from unseen holes. Fewer people. I count only a dozen as Halloway and I jog by. Familiar faces, with all the familiar wear and tear. All of us, hanging together with a little spackle and duct tape.

The Q is a large room right next to the entrance. Used to be a bank vault, maybe. I inherited it from whoever built this compound. A large window is cut in one side. I step up to the thick plexiglass and examine the current occupants. Half a dozen, all dressed in ragged clothes. Even Florez. Easy to pick him out. I can practically feel the high IQ bleed through the window.

I rap the mic against the glass. "What brings you here, Professor?"

Florez rushes to the window and pounds on it. "Please, let us in! We've been on the run for the past six weeks and this is the first—"

"Well, whose fault is that? This cozy little apocalypse we've got going on is courtesy of you guys at Anastasia, right?"

The professor goes still. There are smudges and cracks in his glasses. They look ready to fall apart. So does he. He'd fit right in here.

"I know. And you have every right to hate me." He sucks in a stuttering breath. "Because it was my fault. All of this. It was my idea."

I gape at Halloway. Did I hear Florez right? Most Anies try to hide who they are or at least downplay their involvement. Some days, it seemed like Anastasia hired nothing but janitors. But Florez admits it? My hand drifts toward my gun.

"The process was originally designed for medicinal purposes." Florez won't meet my gaze. "Reinvigorate dying or dead tissue. The possibilities seemed endless. But it was my idea to... well." He sighed. "We had the tissue samples. Why not try it?"

Now my hand is on my gun. It'd be easy to finally get justice for my boy. Just open the door and...

Wait. One of the other survivors doesn't look so good. She stumbles, catching herself against the wall.

Florez notices as well. He turns back to the window, his eyes wide with horror. "Please, let us in! Before it's too late!"

The survivor wretches and doubles over. The color drains from her skin, highlighting the angry red welts peppering her face and arms.

I back away from Q. No way we're letting them in now! I whirl on Halloway. "Get the burn team here. Now!"

He stumbles away, but we both know it's too late. It'll take them three minutes to gear up. Another two to assemble here. Not fast enough. I've seen it happen too many times.

The survivor convulses and her welts tear open. I should retreat, but I only stare. There's a beauty to the flow of the nanofluid, a mesmerizing dance. The ooze easily overtakes the other refugees, including Florez. He beats against the window in a desperate attempt to break through. Does him no good as the goo absorbs him. Once the organic matter is gone, it starts to nibble away at the walls of the chamber. In theory, this process should take a while, but lately, the goo's gotten nastier. Faster. Within a minute, cracks form in the Q as the goo reconfigures the metal. Within another minute, the chamber is gone.

The nanomachines in the goo pull the raw material into a lump, which pulsates as the microscopic builders follow the blueprints in their memory. So what are we going to get this time?

The mass rises up, a large head bursting from the blob. The creature has a thick chest set on massive legs. Tiny forearms claw at the air.

I groan. Not one of these. Not here.

The newly reborn T-Rex stumbles forward. Its skin is a mottle of green and silver, not quite organic but not quite metal, either. Instead of roaring, it groans. I guess it's the dino equivalent of moaning for brains. And it shuffles forward, its beady eyes looking for victims to bite and infect and continue the process of reconquering the planet, reclaiming it for these undead lizards.

The burn team shoves past me, their flamethrowers clattering on their backs. Too late to kill the nanomachines, but maybe they can slow the Rex down long enough for us to evacuate. We'll have to start over, but we can survive this. We have to. Mammals lived in the shadow of the dinosaurs once. We'll do it again.

I hope.

Notes on "In the Shadow"

This is another flash fiction story, one that I sold to my friends who had grown their *Splickety* empire into a couple of spinoff magazines. One of them was *Havok*, a magazine that focused on speculative fiction stories. One month, they were going to do an issue on dinosaur-related stories. And once again, I decided to write a story with a twist to it.

There's not much else to say about this one. The April 2017 issue of *Havok* that this story appeared in also features stories from some friends of mine, like Steve Rzasa and Kerry Nietz. And it has an awesome cover designed by the one and only Kirk DouPonce. Kirk is amazing. He's done some covers for my novels and I think he's the best of the best. And if you want to see something really cool, head over to YouTube and search for "Kirk DouPonce Havok cover." You can see a time-lapse video of how he made this particular cover.

RESOLUTION

THE ONE THING I feared most when Clifford died was living alone. As it turns out, I didn't need to worry. I wasn't alone, but I'm not sure if a mouse invasion counts. But at least the mice were the catalyst that made things better for me.

I shuffled into my living room, shoving my walker in front of me. I hate that thing. I don't need it. I only fell those two times, but ever since then, the doctor has insisted that I use it, even in my own home. I tried to tell him I would be careful, but he didn't listen. Just gave me the look, the same one that I used to get from Clifford. The don't-argue-with-me look.

Like I said, I don't need it. Not really. I'm observant enough without it. I easily spotted the way the throw rug at the bottom of the stairs was rolled up on itself, ready to trip anyone, not just me. I frowned at it. My knees and hips started to ache without even stooping down to deal with it. Well, the walker had to be good for something. I poked at the rug with the walker until it unrolled.

A tiny mouse scampered off the rug and darted between my feet.

I stumbled back a step, coming dangerously close to tumbling over. Wouldn't that be a great thing to tell the doctor! *How did you fall this time, Bonnie? A mouse scared me and I wound up breaking my hip.* He'd ship me off to the home right then and there, and Pete would probably help him too.

The mouse ran for the kitchen, so I grabbed my walker and turned around, following its path. Unfortunately, I was too slow. By the time I made it into the kitchen, there was no sign of the intruder. I stood in the door and glared at the sink, the refrigerator, the stove. If I were a mouse, where would I go?

Something thumped under the stove.

Ah ha! I hustled over to the stove. Once I had braced myself against the counter, I hit it with my walker.

Three mice darted out from under the stove and raced across the floor. They zigged and zagged as if their tails were on fire. One squeezed under the fridge, while the other two wove around each other. They ran next to each other before splitting off. One turned around and slipped back under the stove while the other disappeared beneath the cabinets.

Not good. I gingerly knelt down near the cabinet. My knees screamed in protest the entire way down. Sure enough, I spotted several mouse droppings next to a hole. Apparently I had had house guests for a while and hadn't realized it.

I sighed and pulled myself back up on the walker. I could hear some of Clifford's advice echo in my ears. *Never be afraid to ask for help. To have a friend, you have to be a friend. I'll always be at your side, dear heart.* But he was gone and had been for five years. That really left me with Pete, if he could be bothered to help his grandmother.

I don't know why I expected him to actually answer the phone. I had to leave him two messages in as many days before he finally bothered to call me back. Two days and two nights, during which I could hear the mice under the stove. I knew where they were. I just couldn't get rid of them.

Finally he called me back at 9:00 at night, just when I was thinking of going to bed. Worse, it was clear he was irritated that he had to talk to me. "What is it, Gram?"

No small talk. No questions about how I was. But that's Pete. "I need your help. There are mice in my house." He should have known that already. I mentioned them in both messages.

A long pause. I could hear music in the background, tinny and grating. Playing a videogame, possibly, not even bothering to stop. "Are you sure?"

"Of course I'm sure! I saw three of them myself."

"You did, huh?" He still didn't believe me. "Well, that's not good."

"No. No, it is not."

"So why are you calling me?"

I took a deep breath, closed my eyes. Said a quick prayer to St. Monica. "I was hoping that you would come over and do something about it."

"Why me? I'm not an exterminator."

I could have gone over the usual arguments: he's the nearest family I had left since his father died. My daughter was all the way in Florida. I could have called her, but she'd only be able to sympathize with me before telling me to call Pete.

"Why don't you just go down to the store and get a trap or something?"

I frowned. I could have done that if I still had a car, but the doctor said I couldn't be trusted to drive, so I gave my Olds to Pete. Oh, he promised he'd always be there to help me, but I usually wound up taking Metro Mobility anywhere I needed to go. Even if I took the bus to the store and bought the traps, I would still need help setting them and emptying them.

"Gram, if you can't do that on your own, are you sure you should be living by yourself?"

His words hurt. This wasn't the first time he'd brought that up either. He probably thought that I'd be out of his hair if I shuffled off to some assisted living facility. But this was my home. Mine and Clifford's. I wasn't going to give it up that easily.

"I just...I just really need my grandson's help right now." Tears stung my eyes and I was tempted to start crying. Maybe I could have guilted him into helping. A long shot, certainly, but maybe worth it.

"Gram, I know. But I'm just swamped right now. I've got no time. Look, just call an exterminator, all right? I'm sure Aunt Leslie will be okay with that too."

I winced at his tone. His voice sounded so like Clifford, it was eerie. But at least I knew that Clifford would always help me. *I'll always be at your side, dear heart.*

"Okay." *Change the subject, Bonnie.* "Would you be able to come over for dinner on Sunday? I think I could whip up some ham and sweet potatoes." His favorite growing up, the perfect bait. He used to demand that meal every time he visited. Maybe it'd be enough to...

He sighed, heavy and loud. "I told you, Gram. I'm swamped. No can do. I promise I'll be there for Easter, okay?"

Two months away. Still, it was the best that I'd get: a promise he would forget in a week at the most.

"All right." I mumbled.

"And you'll call the exterminator?"

"I'll...I'll call one."

"Sounds good. Love you, Gram."

And with a click, he was gone. He said he loved me. I wished that I had more evidence than easily spoken words.

The exterminator stood at my front door. He was young, mid twenties. Black. Was that the right word? I could never keep track.

"Name's Julian, ma'am." He set down his case and extended his hand. "Understand you've got some little furry roommates you want evicted."

I stepped out of the way and motioned for him to come in. As he crossed the threshold, I noticed the edge of a tattoo poking up past his collar. Was he safe? Could a convicted felon even become an exterminator?

Julian turned to me and smiled, his eyes twinkling. "Ma'am? Everything okay?"

I took a deep breath and nodded. I was being silly. The company wouldn't have sent him if he was trouble. "Of course. I saw the mice in here."

We headed for the kitchen. I tried to move faster. It wasn't fair to make Julian wait. But he didn't seem to mind. He shuffled along next to me, making nice comments on the pictures in the living room, the paint job on the walls. Very polite.

Once we were in the kitchen, he knelt down and looked at the hole under the cabinet. He nodded. "Not surprised you've got this problem. Mice don't like these Minnesota winters either. They want to get in where it's warm too. Surprised you haven't seen them before now."

I shrugged, unsure of what to say.

"But not to worry, I'll get to work. You just relax here, ma'am, and I'll take care of everything."

And he was off, moving through the house, looking for evidence of the mice, setting out traps and poison and...well, I wasn't entirely sure. He kept up a running commentary, but his words blurred together.

I sighed. How had it come to this? After Clifford died, Leslie and Matthew had been so worried about what would happen to me. They had wanted me to move into White Pines right then and there, but I had insisted that I didn't have to go to an assisted living facility. I could manage this house on my own. I had insisted on it. And they had agreed, albeit reluctantly. But then Matthew had died too, leaving me Pete as my only helper.

Maybe they had been on to something. Maybe it was too much. I wasn't blind. I could see the thin layer of grime that coated the table and counters. It was harder to clean up after myself. And while I had promised Pete ham and sweet potatoes, a good cup of soup was all I could manage most days. The house was probably decaying right along with me.

My gaze hitched on the fridge, which was covered with drawings from Leslie's kids and old photos and newspaper clippings. In the middle of it all was a bright yellow sticky note. I snorted at the sight of it. My New Year's Resolution, the one I had been forced to make.

Esther, my neighbor, had insisted on taking me to the senior center for the New Year's Gala, a fancy term for us old farts sitting around and complaining about grandkids, the price of medication, and the cold weather. We were all supposed to make a New Year's resolution. I didn't want to, but Esther insisted. She even went so far as to not only suggest one, but write it down so I wouldn't forget: "Get out there and meet someone new."

Of course she suggested that. When her Nathan died, she didn't wait long before she latched on to Simon at the senior center as "her new beau," as she put it. She thought all I needed to do is get my hooks into some new fella and everything would be just fine.

But I couldn't do that. What man would want a ninety year old lady half crippled with arthritis? Besides, Clifford and I had been together for sixty-five years. That's not something you replace on a whim. I couldn't just meet someone new and be done with it. Every day was a constant reminder of what I didn't have anymore. Any guy I met was just going to be a faint shadow of the part of me that's buried out at Fort Snelling.

At the rate I was going, though, those mice would have been my only visitors. Only Julian was going to take care of them quickly enough.

But wait. An idea started to form in my mind, a way that maybe Julian could help me keep that resolution after all.

Julian was thorough, checking the basement, plugging all the holes, making sure that everything is taken care of. A few hours after he

arrived, he bustled into the kitchen, tablet in hand. "All right, ma'am. I think we're good to go. You shouldn't see those little pests again. But if you do, you give me a call, okay?"

I smiled at him from my seat at the kitchen table. I had been busy too. A fresh pot of coffee sat in front of me along with a plate of cookies. "Thank you so much. Can I get you a cup of coffee?"

He didn't look up from his computer. "No, thank you, ma'am. Just need your signature and a check and I'll be out of your hair."

Oh. I glanced at the snack, then at him. He didn't seem to notice that I'd put it together. Or care, apparently. I sighed and hauled myself out of the chair, snaring my walker so I could get to my purse on the counter. I fished out my checkbook and tottered back to the table. My handwriting was more squiggle than fluid loops, but I managed to scratch in all the right details, including my scraggly signature.

Julian accepted the check and had me scribble my name on his tablet using my finger. I glared at the thing. Pete probably had one of those too. Then he nodded to me and headed for the front door.

I collapsed in my chair, staring at the plate of cookies. It wasn't anything special, but I had hoped that maybe...

And then he was back, chuckling to himself. "I'm sorry, ma'am. Forgot my kneepads in here and..." He paused next to me, his eyes suddenly warm. "Are you okay?"

I tried to nod, but I could feel the tears welling up in my eyes. I turned away from him. Last thing I wanted was some stranger's pity.

He cleared his throat. "You know what? You were my last call today. A little coffee sounds pretty good." He slid into the seat across from me and looked around the kitchen. "So have you always lived here?"

I shook my head. "I grew up in Hastings. How about you?"

"Nah, I'm a transplant from Kansas City. Moved up here for college, wound up doing this instead."

"Do you like it?"

"Pays the bills." He looked at the cookies. "These for me too?"

I nodded, and he took three of them. "So I saw a bunch of pictures of your husband. What did he do?"

Now if this were one of those smarmy Hallmark movies, Julian and I would have become fast friends and he'd be a regular at my table. But that didn't happen. That was the only time I ever saw him. But I realized that day that even though he was gone, Clifford's advice still rang true. I could ask for help, and if it wouldn't come from Pete, I could hire someone to help me a little around the house. If I wanted a friend, I had to be one first. And even though he wasn't there physically, Clifford was still at my side and always would be.

NOTES ON "RESOLUTION"

WHAT IS THIS STORY even doing in here? I mean, up until now, all of my short stories have fallen under the speculative fiction umbrella. We have some fantasy, some science fiction, some horror, some urban fantasy. Why do we have this story about a sweet old lady making a friend with an exterminator.

Well, allow me to explain:

Back in 2017, I learned about a short story writing contest called The Short Story Challenge. It's put on by an organization called NYC Midnight, and the rules are wild. There are four rounds that take place over an entire year. In the first round, the participants are given a genre and two story prompts that must be included in the story. They then have a week to draft, write, and revise a short story that can't be longer than 2,500 words. All of the participants are grouped into heats that share the same genre and prompts. Once the stories are submitted, they're judged and the top five entries from each heat move on to the second round.

This sounded like a blast, so I decided to enter. And for round one, I was asked to write a drama about a New Years Eve resolution that featured an exterminator. I had a week. Go.

I have to admit, I panicked when I first saw what I had. I'm a speculative fiction guy! I don't do dramas! But once I calmed down, I thought it through and I remembered something that a parishioner used to tell my wife: "To have a friend you have to be a friend." And once I remembered that, the rest of it clicked into place. I sat down and banged out this story and sent it off. Apparently the judges liked it, because I was able to move on to the next round...

SPLINTERS

SPLINTERS OF SUNLIGHT SLOWLY cooked Melanie's skin. After a life spent on Dixon hab, she wasn't used to the full spectrum of planetary light. She glared up at the pale blue star. Why did they have to come to Flosie 8AD3 for their school trip? Why couldn't they have gone somewhere fun?

"Hey, how can you tell that cricks are religious? Because they're always preying on you!"

Rabbani Daher laughed at his own joke. Melanie giggled in spite of herself, then swallowed a groan. Why couldn't she have been paired up with someone other than Rabbani? Like Lincoln, her chemistry partner. This trip could have been an opportunity to get him alone and maybe let him know how she felt. But no, she was stuck with Rabbani. So where was Lincoln?

Before she could find him in the crowd, Mr. V motioned for them to gather. "What did you think of the qrosyd settlement?"

Melanie rolled her eyes. Only their teacher would call the crick "qrosyd." It had been his idea to come here, to take a tour of an actual crick settlement.

And yet Mr. V had insisted that they had so much more to learn from their defeated enemy. So their class had trudged through a city that looked like a bunch of crumbling dirt spires dotted with holes and riddled with cracks. If this was really the race that had conquered a quarter of the galaxy before they attacked the humans ten years earlier, Melanie was not impressed.

A few of her classmates offered up half-hearted observations. They were just parroting back stuff that Mr. V had said on the shuttle ride, but he still beamed like they had offered him deep insights.

"Very good." He clapped his hands. "We have one more stop before we leave, a real treat. Follow me!"

He led them to a shallow pit ringed by low stone benches then motioned for the class to take a seat. As Melanie plopped down on a rock, she looked for Lincoln. Where was he?

Then she spotted him, his arm around Leala Pechin. A wave of cold needles swept over Melanie. Wasn't Leala dating Richard Belmont? Apparently not anymore, given how entangled she was with Lincoln.

And why wouldn't he pick Leala over her, what with Leala's silky blond hair and flawless skin. Melanie was a crick by comparison, with mousy brown hair and skin that still erupted with acne in spite of all the treatments she could find. Leala had curves where Melanie's body was mostly straight lines. Why had she ever thought that Lincoln would want her?

"Greetings!"

Several of her classmates gasped and Melanie turned toward the pit. A crick stared up at them. It was short, no more than a meter tall. Thick chitinous armor covered its body. The alien rattled as it walked on its hind four legs. Four translucent wings vibrated as it moved and rainbows danced over their surface.

"We are pleased that you have honored us with your presence." Its voice rasped and clicked, like pebbles being shaken in a metal can. "We wish to bestow honor on you as well. My brood will perform a sacred dance. This would normally be performed before a war, but we are at peace, yes? This dance requires at least fifty qrosyd, but we no longer have the numbers to perform this properly. Thus we will be using holographic substitutes for this reenactment."

A dozen crick crawled out of a nearby structure and filled the pit. One of them carried a holoprojector, which it left next to their spokesbug. They positioned themselves at various spots in the ring, their heads facing in. The leader stepped over to the projector and fiddled with it.

A low hum filled the air and suddenly, dozens of crick flickered into existence. They were clearly holograms, given the way that their bodies were somewhat translucent and wavered in the bright sunlight.

If the crick noticed the problems, they didn't let on. Instead, they rubbed their back legs together, creating an eerie, droning melody. The real crick and recreations danced and wove, leaping over one another and undulating their appendages, wings, and antennae as they moved.

A few of the students laughed, but Melanie actually enjoyed the performance. It was strange but the crick moved with such fluid grace, their motions perfectly synchronized. It was like waves skimming the top of a dark ocean, the trilling music sucking her in as it pulsated and thrummed.

But then smoke erupted from the projector and most of the dancers vanished. The lead crick rushed to the machine and worked on it, but it was too late. The dance stuttered to a halt.

Rabbani guffawed. Some of the other students laughed too. Even Lincoln smiled, whispering something into Leala's ear that made her giggle. But Melanie actually felt sorry for the crick. She knew how embarrassed she'd be if this happened to her.

The crick turned to the class. "My apologies. We are unused to this technology. I'm afraid the performance is over."

Mr. V stood and faced the students. "Well, let's get going. Maybe we'll get a chance to peek into the hatchery and see the next generation of qrosyd being born."

The class groaned but they dutifully filed out of the pit. Lincoln wrapped his arm around Leala, but as he did, his gaze caught on Melanie. He smiled and winked.

Her stomach dropped into her feet. How could he do that? Didn't he know how she felt about him? Tears stung her eyes and she realized that if she kept going on the tour, she was likely going to lose it.

Mr. V stepped up next to her. "Melanie? Is everything all right?"

She forced herself to nod. "Yes. I...I'm just a little tired. Can I rest here for a moment?"

He frowned, casting a look at the qrosyd, who were arguing in a series of hisses and clicks. "I suppose so. Just don't dawdle for too long."

"I won't. I promise."

The rest of the class left. Melanie tucked her knees under her chin. Maybe they would forget about her, leave her here. The way she was feeling, that wouldn't be too bad. Let her rot with the rest of the crick, their buildings, and—

"Excuse me. Your friends have left."

Melanie looked up. A crick stood next to her.

"I'm sorry. Do I need to leave?" she asked.

"No. In fact, I wish to ask you a question. What did you think? We have not performed that dance in many years. Was it acceptable?"

Melanie smiled. "It was really good." And much to her surprise, she really meant it. "I liked the music and your dance was really interesting."

"A shame you could not see the entire dance."

"That is too bad."

"But perhaps..." The crick studied her. "Would you care for a different experience? One that is more reliable?"

"Uh...sure?"

The crick produced a small red box, a series of lights dancing across its surface. "This is of qrosyd design, so is more dependable. With this, you will see this colony as it was before the foolishness of war." The crick set the box next to her and pressed its top. "Relax and enjoy."

A soft whine wove around her. And then the bottom fell out of Melanie's mind.

She stood in the settlement, only now it gleamed in the sun. The buildings weren't piles of dirt but pillars of light reaching up for the stars themselves. And the colony bustled with life, hundreds of cricks moving through the streets with orderly purpose. There, a nanny with hundreds of grubs clinging to her carapace. There, a regiment of soldiers, marching in straight lines, ready to defend the colony from any intruders. And the music! As the cricks spoke to one another, their voices blended and wove together into a rich melody that resonated deep within Melanie's chest. She could feel the purpose burning in her, to build, to nurture, to savor.

Melanie lurched forward, the vision disappearing from her mind. She turned to the qrosyd, tears in her eyes. "So beautiful..."

"It was, once. But in our folly, we attacked your people and you proved the stronger. Now all that is left to us is splinters." The qrosyd looked up at her. "You had best be going. I believe your tour is leaving soon."

They were? Melanie turned around and saw Mr. V standing at the entrance to the pit, tapping his watch. She quickly hurried after her teacher.

The rest of the class was lined up at the shuttle. When she saw Lincoln with Leala, it didn't hurt as much. Not after what she had witnessed. Her lost opportunity with him was small compared to the qrosyd's lost grandeur.

Rabbani sidled up next to her. "Hey, Mel! How many cricks does it take to change a plasma converter?"

"Shut up." She shoved her way past him onto the shuttle and found her seat.

Her classmates chattered, but she tuned them out, choosing to stare out the window at the settlement. She couldn't stop, even as the shuttle lifted off. She would never forget. She would carry the melody with her forever.

He watched the human shuttle climb out of the atmosphere with a grim sense of satisfaction. No more tours were scheduled for today, which was just as well. The sower needed time to regenerate.

"Well? What did it plant this time?"

He resisted the urge to snap at his subordinate. The younger generations were losing their way. They had been since the mammals defeated them.

"Let us find out."

They left the pit and headed for the hive's entrance. The humans had never found this entrance, queen be praised. He descended into the tunnels, into the lab, where the weavers worked to secure their future. He surrendered the sower to one of the attendants, who pushed the now inert cube into its slot in the mainframe.

A holographic image of the girl appeared over the device. It was all he could do to keep from spitting bile at it. To think that they had to suffer such filth! But it would be worth it. He studied the collected data. The scans revealed a typical human, vacuous and flighty. But her neural imprint suggested an aptitude for chemistry.

He twisted his mandibles in delight. Usually the humans had negligible skills, nothing the qrosyd could use. But every now and then, they found one like this. Fertile soil for their splinters. The girl wouldn't notice at first, but eventually, her thoughts would be consumed with justice for the qrosyd. And those thoughts would grow into actions. With her skills and knowledge...

"Not another bomb maker," the subordinate said. "We don't need terrorists, we need soldiers."

He rounded on her and slashed at her face. To her credit, she backed out of the chamber.

How little she understood. War had failed them. It had left them with only splinters. But each one of those could be driven into the minds of their enemies and soon, those would be forged into a spear that could stab deep into their enemies' heart.

Playing the fool for the humans now was a small price. With patience, the qrosyd would rise again.

NOTES ON "SPLINTERS"

THIS WAS ROUND TWO for the Short Story Challenge of 2017. The second round worked very similarly to the first: all participants were grouped into new heats and given the same genre and two story prompts, only this time, our stories couldn't be longer than 2,000 words and we had only three days to draft, write, and revise the stories. I was so relieved when I saw that my genre was science fiction, but it had to be a story that included a walking tour and a reenactor. Cue the panicked brainstorming! But as I thought about it, the story of the Cricks came into focus and, since I'm still a big fan of twist endings, I decided to include the ending.

I like how this story turned out. The judges, however, did not. This was as far as I made it in 2017, but I was hooked. I knew I had to participate the next year. So when 2018 rolled around, I was quick to sign up...

THE SWEETEST INDULGENCE

"IT'S ALL ABOUT MODERATION. It's not that he can't indulge once in a while, but be more...judicious about when he has sweets."

Even as I said the words, I knew I was wasting my breath. Erik Dearborn looked like he belonged on one of the pamphlets that hung in a rack on my office wall about the need for healthy eating: immaculate blond hair, expensive clothing, and...what's a nice word for it? On the larger side? Chubby? The only difference was that the models smiled, even though they were pretending to have childhood obesity and type 1 diabetes. Erik's face seemed frozen in a perpetual scowl. At least, I think it was. He hadn't even looked up from his iPhone once since sulking into my office. I frowned. Who gives an eight-year-old an iPhone?

My gaze slid to the left and I had my answer. Michelle McGhee, Erik's mom, was clearly a stereotypically overwhelmed single mom. Her brown hair was in a frizzed-out ponytail, and her makeup couldn't quite hide the dark bags under her blue eyes. I sympathized with her. The single part, not the mom part.

Not by choice, of course. After all, I'm the woman who DVRs Hallmark movies for weekend binges and would eat those chalky hearts year-round if I didn't know how empty their calories were.

I'm a 43-year-old walking irony—a die-hard romantic ignored by love all my life.

Come to think of it, there's probably a Hallmark movie—or ten—with that exact premise. The question is whether or not I should keep hoping for my own happy ending.

I blinked. C'mon, Laura, focus.

I glanced down at Erik's chart. Not that I needed the review; I knew the case well enough. Every couple of months, Ms. McGhee would beg us for help because her son was being teased at school or she had seen some news report that spooked her. Then her pediatrician would confirm that yes, Erik was slightly overweight and no, he hadn't developed any health issues yet. And I'd deliver another lecture on the food pyramid and the importance of limiting snacks. They'd go home, ignore everything, and the whole cycle would start over.

Might as well keep up the song and dance. "I understand that it may be easier to give in when—"

"Mom, we're going to Dairy Queen after we're done, right?" Erik didn't even look up from his phone.

I glanced at Michelle, my eyebrow quirked. Now was as good a time as any for her to grow a backbone.

She squirmed in her seat. "Honey, I don't know if that's—"

Erik's eyes practically spit fire. "But you *promised!*"

"I know I did, but maybe we should start thinking about—"

"No, you said that if I went to this stupid appointment, we could get Blizzards afterwards. Were you just trying to trick me?"

Michelle looked to me for support. I motioned for her to keep going. It was difficult, but this would be good for both of them in the long run.

Before she could say anything, though, Erik went in for the kill. "You said that you would never lie to me the way *he* used to!"

Low blow, kid.

Michelle paled. Tears wetted her eye. Erik had the nerve to smirk at her. She gathered up her things. Apparently the appointment was over.

Erik eyed the candy dish I kept on my desk. He jutted his chin at it. "Can I have some?"

I gaped at him. Really?

Michelle's eyes quietly pleaded with me.

Fine. "You may have..."

His hand dropped into the bowl like a steam shovel's claw, scooping out half the bowl.

"...one."

Erik stomped out of my office, somehow managing to unwrap a candy while still staring at his phone. I considered offering a prayer to St. Helena that the twerp would walk into my door frame, but that would only end with crocodile tears until mom promised more junk food. He flicked the wrapper off his fingertips and the cellophane floated to the floor.

I hauled myself out of my chair and went over to scoop it up. Michelle and Erik went down the hall, the little brat complaining all the while that my candy supply sucked. I smirked to myself. Sugar free mints, kid.

Then a conference door opened and Dr. Armstrong stepped into the hallway, almost colliding with Michelle. The two danced around each other, his arms out and open, almost like he was expecting her to fall. He smiled, a flash of teeth that might've caused my knees to turn to jelly if I were twenty years younger. Oh, there was no doubt Dr. Armstrong was handsome, with those ice blue eyes and that chiseled jawline.

Of course, I tend to prefer brown eyes. And I'd take a crooked nose or mysterious scar any day over a picture-perfect profile. A face that hints at life, at a rich backstory to be read and savored.

So no, unlike half the nurses who'd started buzzing the moment Dr. Armstrong joined our staff last week, I wouldn't cast him in my personal Hallmark movie. Michelle, on the other hand...

Dr. Armstrong said something to Michelle and she laughed, her eyes brightening for the first time since she arrived at the clinic. He touched her arm, then stepped away and allowed her to pass. Michelle followed Erik, but she looked over her shoulder at him one last time.

My eyes widened. That's what Erik needed! Not a diet, but a dad! Michelle had been single as long as I knew her and office rumors said that Dr. Armstrong was a recent divorcee too. My eyes widened. If there was just some way to get the two of them together...

"Excuse me, *Senora* West? You need me to pick up those wrappers for you?"

Huh? I turned around. Miguel, one of the janitors, smiled at me. I smiled back. Miguel always had a way of brightening my day. He would wave to me when I passed the staff break room in the morning and be the last to bid me a good night when work was done.

He nodded toward the hallway. Apparently Erik had left empty mint wrappers like a trail of breadcrumbs down the hall.

"Oh, no, Miguel. I can do that."

"Nah, I got this. That's what they pay me for, right?" He scooped up one of the wrappers. As he straightened, he looked down the hall. "Checking out Doc Armstrong, eh? Very handsome!"

I didn't answer. He studied my face, then shrugged, picking up another wrapper. "Have a good day, *caramelita*."

Oh, I would. The whole reason why I became a dietitian in the first place was to change peoples' lives for the better. And if I could get Michelle and Dr. Armstrong together, I'd count that as a win.

The next morning, I was ready to go. I would call Michelle and tell her I was referring Erik's case to a specialist. Then I would casually bump into Dr. Armstrong and grease the skids a little. Talk about how I was sending him a new patient, how his mom had been alone for a while. Once in the same room, biology would take over. They definitely had a moment in the hallway. All I had to do was make sure they had another one and soon.

As I slipped into my office, I noticed a new bag of mints on my desk. Where did that come from? I shrugged and stashed it in my desk, then got ready for my first appointment. After all, I didn't want to call first thing. No, it had to look like I had taken the time to consult with my colleagues first.

But by noon, I was practically vibrating in my chair with anticipation. I found Michelle's cell number in Erik's chart. Hopefully she'd be on her lunch break.

"Hello?"

I bit back an excited squeal. "Michelle? This is Laura West from Purpose Health Clinic. Do you have a moment?"

"Uh, sure."

"Well, I was thinking about Erik's case after you left, and I think maybe you...*he* would benefit from seeing a new specialist. His name is Dr. Armstrong and I think you guys would really hit it off. I mean, I think that Erik would be able to relate to him. Better, I mean. I know you've been seeing Dr. Odette for a while, but let's be honest, while Sheila is wonderful, there are just some things that a boy needs to talk to a man about, you know?"

"...okay. What's his specialty?"

Smoldering eyes and broad shoulders.

"Uh..." Shoot. I should have known she'd ask and I couldn't re-member. I frantically dug through the papers on my desk to find the staff directory. "Well, he's..." There it was! I quickly thumbed through it and discovered his specialty was... "Obstetrics?"

Oh no! I covered my mouth. Did I say that out loud?

"You think the solution to my son's eating problems is to send him to an OB/GYN?"

I swallowed a groan. Maybe I could salvage this. "I know it's un-orthodox, but Dr. Armstrong would have some unique insight into your situation, and..."

"Look, Ms. West, I know Erik can be a bit difficult at times, but that's no reason for you to tease me like this."

What? No! "That's not what I was trying to do at all. I really think—"

The line went dead with a click. I set the phone down and groaned into my hands. That didn't work.

But I couldn't give up. Maybe I could arrange for Dr. Armstrong to show up in my office the next time Michelle brought Erik in? Oh, who was I kidding? There was no way she would be coming to see me anytime soon.

That left me with only one option.

I found a scrap of paper and scribbled down Michelle's number, along with "Call me" encircled by a heart. I toyed with the idea of kissing the paper, but I hadn't worn bright enough lipstick to make it work. Now I just needed to deliver the invitation.

As I slipped out of my office, I ran into Miguel. Literally. He grabbed my arms and steadied me.

"Hold on, *caramelita*. Don't be so rushed." He smiled at me, a brilliant flash of teeth. "Did you get the candies I left for you?"

Oh, that was him? "Yes, I did. Thank you."

He studied my face. But his grin shifted into something forced. "Well, don't let me keep you."

He squeezed my arms and then slunk off down the hall. What was that about? I couldn't puzzle over his odd behavior, though. I was on a mission.

Thankfully, Dr. Armstrong wasn't in his office. Better yet, his door was unlocked too. And best yet, his leather jacket was slung over the back of his chair. Perfect! I folded up the fake note from Michelle and slipped it into the pocket and retreated to my office before he came back.

This would work. I could just picture it now: Dr. Armstrong would find the note and give Michelle a call. It would be awkward, but they would hit it off. Now all I had to do was sit back and wait for the sparks to fly.

The sparks flew, all right. And they wound up setting me on fire.

As it turned out, the office scuttlebutt was wrong. Dr. Armstrong wasn't a divorcee. He wasn't even separated. And his wife found the note. That discovery led to a three hour verbal brawl that only ended when their neighbors called the cops. So he was really curious as to how that phone number got into his pocket, as was the clinic's administration. When they called the number, Michelle told them about my "disturbing" phone call. I tried to explain what I was doing. What's the harm in trying to encourage two people to find love?

Well, apparently when that encouragement violates HIPAA privacy laws, it's enough to get you fired.

As I worked on packing up my office, I thought about my options. I would be okay. I had only been at Purpose for three years. I could find another job.

With a groan, I banged my head on my desk. Who was I kidding? I lectured people about moderation and taking small steps. So much for caution! And now my office decor was stuffed into a cardboard box and I would have to make a walk of shame past gossipy coworkers. They'd be telling stories about how I wrecked my career for years. Not to mention Dr. Armstrong's marriage! What was I going to do?

Someone knocked gently on my door. Miguel leaned against my door frame, a sad smile on his face. "Heard what happened, *Senora* West. Got to say, it's not going to be the same coming to work and you not being here. They really take that privacy stuff seriously, huh?"

"And for good reason." I tried to force a laugh and it came out more of a cough. "Can't have crazy people stealing phone numbers out of the medical records."

"Oh, I don't know." He took a step into the office. "I understand why you did it. Everyone's gotta have someone, right? What's the harm in trying to make people happy?" He nodded toward the box on my desk. "You ever open those mints I got you?"

Oh, of course. I guess I didn't need them anymore since I didn't have a desk to put a candy dish on. I rummaged through the box and found the bag, then held it out to him.

He chuckled, a throaty, rich sound. "You didn't look at them, did you?"

I frowned and examined the bag. How had I missed the sticky note on there? A message, written in meticulous letters: "What are after dinner mints without dinner first?" And a phone number too. With Miguel's looping signature.

My mouth popped open. When had he sat down on the edge of my desk? When had his eyes become so warm and inviting, such a rich, deep brown that sent a delicious tremor through my stomach. Why hadn't I ever noticed how handsome he was? Like a mix between George Clooney and Antonio Banderas! The perfect leading man for my own story!

"Do you think there's any rule against former coworkers going out to get a bite to eat?" he whispered.

I giggled. "No, I don't think so."

"Good. How about tomorrow night?"

"I think my schedule is free."

"'Til then, *caramelita*."

He favored me with one more enticing smile and then backed out the door. I clenched my fists and a laugh bubbled up my throat. Moderation may be good most of the time, but every now and then, it was okay to indulge. And love was the sweetest treat of all.

NOTES ON "THE SWEETEST INDULGENCE"

So in 2018, I entered The NYC Short Story Challenge again. My first round assignment? A romantic comedy that had to do with spoiling a child and featured a dietitian.

Cue panic.

I had no idea how to write a romance story. There is a running joke at the OYAN conference that "when you think romance, you think John Otte." It's a joke I made in 2016 at the first conference I taught at. The students picked up on it and ran with it. But all you have to do is ask my wife: when you think romance, the last person you think of is me. And now I had to write a romcom?

Once again, after a day to panic, I was able to sit down and cobble together a basic story. And then, I kind of cheated. I contacted one of my friends who writes romantic comedy books and asked her to take a peek at what I had put together. She gave me some valuable feedback that allowed me to create the story you just read.

Thanks to Melissa Tagg, I made it through round one that year. So what was waiting for me?

ONE FINAL ADVENTURE

I EXAMINED MY TARGET. The Monastery of the Deep was a squat fortress perched on a rocky island. The monks rarely received visitors, their isolation enforced by the lack of a physical drawbridge. Instead, a mageroad could be conjured from the monastery's gate to the mainland if the monks felt friendly. I wasn't likely to find such hospitality in the middle of the night, though.

My stomach flipped. Why was I so nervous? I had done crazier things than this in my eighteen years: battling the fire golems of Kazzak in an active volcano, facing off against ogres in Felguard Pass, or gliding with the hawkmen of Eyer. This felt more dangerous.

But then it wasn't every day that I tried to prevent a treaty from being signed by two warring kingdoms. In two days' time, the citizens of both Terria and Collu would come together to witness the ratification of a peace treaty that would be solemnized by the marriage of Terria's crown prince to one of Collu's princesses. Due to the importance of the occasion, the Orb of Terria would be taken from the monastery to bless the new marriage.

Except I was going to steal the Orb tonight. No Orb, no wedding, and, I guessed, no treaty. The theft would be my final hurrah, my last adventure. After all, Father had been nagging me to stop risking my life on these ridiculous capers. One way or another, tonight would be the end.

Focus, Zek. You've got this.

By my reckoning, the monastery was a quarter mile away, separated from the mainland by frothing waves. That, plus the beasts that lurked in the dark waters, made approaching the island on the water nigh impossible. But that wasn't my plan.

I loaded my crossbow with a special grappling hook. In its tip was a small magacite crystal. I had paid quite a bit to have the proper spell cast into the crystal, but now it would pay off. Taking careful aim at the monastery, I pictured the closest gargoyle that overlooked the harbor so the spell knew where to go, then fired.

Just as the arrow was about to drop toward the waves, the spell within the magacite flared to life and homed in on the gargoyle, dragging a length of rope behind it. The arrow struck home a second later. I pulled the rope taut around the tree. Now came the fun part.

I hopped onto the rope and give it an experimental bounce. Then I took one careful step after another. Sure, I could have just shimmied across, but where was the excitement in that? If this was my final adventure, I was going to do it with style!

The wind was chaotic, slamming into me from multiple sides. I almost lost my balance and pitched into the waters more times than I wanted to admit. But I kept breathing the way I had been taught, stayed focused on the objective, and before I knew it, I made it to the ledge next to the gargoyle.

Finding an open window was easy enough. The monks trusted their isolation too much. The room I crawled into was unoccupied, so I borrowed a robe that hung on the back of the door for a disguise. I slipped through the halls until I arrived at the inner sanctum. After glancing around to make sure I wouldn't be spotted, I set to work on the lock. I didn't expect to have much difficulty with it. Again, the monks were too trusting. But I was surprised to discover the door was unlocked. I frowned, my stomach twisting more. This seemed too fortunate. But I couldn't ignore the opportunity. I crept inside.

The central sanctum was magnificent, as ornate as I remembered it. The walls were covered in gilt panels, depicting the foundation of Terria by the Gods Below themselves. And there, at the back of the room, was a dais with the Orb itself. This close, it looked unimpressive, like a simple hunk of glass. It certainly didn't seem like the holiest object in the kingdom.

I hesitated in the doorway because I knew the monks had worked numerous wards and curses into the sanctum. But I had a magacite crystal prepared for this obstacle as well, one that would dispel anything that might stop me.

I fished the crystal out of my pocket and held it out. The mage had said that the crystal would glow in the presence of wards before disarming them. But the stone remained inert in my hand. I frowned, then took a tentative step forward. Still nothing. Another step. The stone remained dull. Had someone already removed the wards?

As I considered what to do next, I heard the rustle of cloth behind me and the whisper of a blade being pulled from a leather sheath.

"I wouldn't do that if I were you," I said. "The monks get awfully cross if someone messes up the floors."

I turned and found myself face to face with someone wearing black clothing, fabric wrapped around his head. He dropped into a ready crouch, the dagger up and ready. He beckoned for me to fight.

Well, who was I to disappoint him?

I launched myself at him, feinting to the right but jabbing with my left. He ducked my obvious attack, dancing out of the way. I dodged a slash, then managed to sweep his legs out from under him. He hit the floor, but then bounced back up again.

Impressive. And as we fought, my admiration for this masked man only grew. He was my equal in terms of brawling. But I proved a challenge to him as well. He only managed to slice my bicep and I was able to land a few punches. But as enjoyable as our sparring was, I knew I had to finish before the monks discovered we were here.

There! An opening. I jumped forward and snared the man's mask, trying to twist it around to block his sight. But the fabric unwound in my hand and he pulled free...

...only to reveal crystalline blue eyes. Thick blond hair fell free, framing a porcelain face that was achingly beautiful.

The other thief was a woman? And not much older than me, by the look of her.

She took advantage of my distraction to plant a kick to my chest. I slammed into one of the panels, which teetered and then fell with a resounding crash. A shout went up in the hallway outside. I bit off a curse. So much for stealth.

The woman tossed something at me and a magacite crystal thumped into my chest. The crystal flared with blue light and suddenly, my arms were pinned at my side. I struggled against the magical energy that held me, but it was no use.

She shot a look at the orb, then back at the door again, as if weighing her options. Then she sighed, threw me a kiss, and scampered up one of the walls and ducking into a small opening. I chuckled. Why didn't I think to use the heating vents like that? *Very* impressive.

A dozen monks thundered into the sanctum, each armed with a quarterstaff or cudgel. When they saw me lying on the floor, they came up short and stared. Then the crowd parted as someone walked through them. He was an imposing man, towering above everyone else, with a stern face framed by a black beard. The monks bowed as he passed, showing the proper reverence to Thazar, king of Terria.

"I should have known you'd try something like this." The king's voice was a low rumble.

I grimaced. "Hello, Father."

He ignored me, instead turning to one of the monks. "Fetch the abbot and see if he can undo the spell holding my son. And then keep him under guard until the ceremony." He spared me a glance. "Let's make sure the crown prince doesn't duck his obligation."

The monk nodded and Father strode out of the sanctum. I sighed, thudding my head against the floor. Sure, the monks would likely be able to set me free. But all they were doing was freeing me from one trap so I could get caught by another.

From the noise outside the monastery, half the kingdom had shown up to enjoy the treaty ratification ceremony. And why wouldn't they? It wasn't like they were the ones getting married.

The monks had done exactly what Father wanted. I had been their "honored guest" with my own "personal attendants" who stuck by my side until the day of the ceremony. That morning, a burly monk made sure I got dressed in a silk outfit that made me look like a strutting peacock. Soon thereafter, Father arrived to inspect me. He too was wearing his ridiculous finery, although on him, it actually looked somewhat decent. He examined me head to toe, then nodded.

"Try not to embarrass the kingdom, will you?" he asked.

I scowled at him.

He sighed. "Believe it or not, Zekarias, I am sorry. I wish it didn't have to be this way, but—"

"Then don't make me marry what's-her-name! I've never even met her!"

"We don't have any choice, son. The Colluans insisted. This is the way we can finally end the war."

"But there hasn't been a battle in over three years!"

"That's only because we've had a truce while we negotiated the treaty. If this falls through, blood will be spilled once again. Is that what you want?"

No, of course not. "But being forced into a marriage?"

"It was the only way they would agree to all the terms of the treaty." He settled his hand on my shoulder. "If it's any consolation, from what I understand, the Princess Ellura isn't thrilled about this situation either. She's been most...insistent about her displeasure."

Oh, perfect! From the way Father patted my shoulder, I knew further protests would be worthless. I was stuck.

But as I thought about it, I realized that I had to go through with it. How many soldiers had died on both sides? My unhappiness in a loveless marriage was a small price to pay to stop the fighting for good. It was like Father had told me. It was time stop adventuring and grow up. For the good of the kingdom, like a prince should.

I sighed. "Let's get this over with, then."

Father led me out of the monastery across the sparkling mageroad and to the pavilion that had been erected for just this occasion. Standing in the center was the King and Queen of Collu. Father and the Colluan king took turns giving short speeches, in which they outlined their hopes for peace between our two kingdoms. I didn't really listen.

Instead, I studied my soon-to-be mother-in-law. Based on what I saw, at least my wife would probably be pretty. That was some comfort, but not much.

Then the King of Collu gestured toward me. "And so it is with great pleasure that we seal this newfound peace between our kingdoms by joining our families together. Prince Zekarias will now marry my daughter, Princess Ellura."

He stepped aside. The crowd behind him parted and a young woman walked toward me. At first, all I could see was her dress, covered in tiny crystals that threw the sun in blinding rays. But as she drew closer, I forced myself to look at her face. Her beautiful, porcelain face, framed by honey blond hair, and...and...

...the most crystalline blue eyes I had ever seen.

My breath caught in my throat as Ellura and I stared at each other. Then recognition spread across her face and she smirked at me.

I chuckled. Maybe this wasn't the end of anything but the start of a new and better adventure.

Notes on "One Final Adventure"

Round two in 2018 for me was a fantasy story involving a treaty and a daredevil. I felt more at ease with this one, seeing as I was a speculative fiction author. So I used the three days I had to draft, write, and revise the story. Again, because of my love of twists, I included the twist ending. I sent it off to the judges, feeling pretty good with myself.

And that's as far as I made it in 2018. I was a little surprised by this one. I thought I did pretty good, but the judges' decision was final.

It was shortly after I found out I didn't make it any farther that I decided to put together the original anthology, and this seemed like a good note to end on. But does this mean that it's the end of my short story career? Not exactly. I've continued to enter the NYC Midnight Short Story Challenge every year. And every now and then, I get the odd hankering to dip my toe into a short story.

Does that mean we'll ever return to the Bewilderness? Time will tell.

Acknowledgements

I've thanked a lot of people for their help and support over the past several years and the list hasn't changed all that much:

To my wonderful wife, who supports these crazy flights of fancy with a lot more patience and grace than I probably deserve.

To my sons, who encourage me in their own unique ways.

To my long-suffering agent, who gives me sage counsel and advice that I usually don't listen to all that well.

To my friend, Jill Williamson, who got me hooked up with the folks who wanted *Night Queen* in the first place.

To the many editors who have worked with me on these projects over the years.

To Megan Edlin, who let me steal the title.

To my family and friends for not giving up on me.

And most of all, to God who often meets me when I get lost in the bewilderness.

ALSO BY

The Failstate Series

Failstate

Gauntlet Goes to Prom (ebook exclusive)

Failstate: Legends

Kynetic: On Target (ebook exclusive)

Failstate: Nemesis

The Ministrix Duology

Numb

The Hive

The Legacy of Ink Trilogy

Drawn in Ash

The Storm's Eye (ebook exclusive)

Drawn through Blood

Cage and the Outpost of Monolith (short story)

Anthologies

Into the Bewilderness
Just Dumb Enough (Contributor)
The Memory Eater (Contributor)
Spirited: 13 Haunting Tales (Contributor)